The Earl's Passionate Plot

Susan Gee Heino

ISBN: 978-0-9886175-7-5

Dedication

To Jack. Again.
No matter what life throws our way,
you're always the man with a plan.
I'm still in awe.

Chapter 1

Hampshire, England, April 1817

"What do you mean, I cannot stay here? This is where I live," Mariah Langley said, blinking back the prickling tears that she simply would not allow her guest to see. "Renford Hall has been our home since... since I was five years old. My step-father's will is most clear on the matter. How can it possibly be that we have no claim here?"

"I understand your confusion, Miss, and I'm sorry."

The weary solicitor removed his spectacles and rubbed the bridge of his nose. Indeed, it was very likely the man had developed a headache as she'd pelted him with questions. No headache he could possibly have, though, would in any way compare to the ache inside her soul as she was forced to hear his words.

"Your step-father was mistaken, Miss Langley. He did not own the property outright. It remains part of the entail of the Earl of Dovington."

"But that can't be. Step-Papa purchased it from the earl years ago. You see the paperwork there, laid out in front of you. You have to be mistaken, Mr. Milson."

"I wish I were, miss. But it seems the earl misrepresented things when he entered that agreement with your step-father. The paperwork is fraudulent, to be blunt. Mr. Renford's ownership could be considered, in actuality, nothing more than a life-lease."

"But he purchased the property when he married my mother. It has been our home all these twenty years!"

"And no doubt he believed his so-called title to it was valid. But it was not. I'm so sorry, miss, but the Earl of Dovington entered into an agreement he was not allowed by law to make. When your step-father died, this property clearly reverted back to the estate."

"But my step-father has been gone three full years now and this is the first I'm hearing of this."

"No one knew about it, I'm afraid. The old earl was not very... conscientious. He was far more interested in drink than in managing his affairs and... well, to be honest, Miss Langley, he was not a pleasant man to be around and for the last few years of his life he did not even have a steward to oversee matters for him. At his passing, things were in a sorry state, indeed. It has taken the new earl more than a full year to sort through the tangle of legal matters and unpaid bills his father left behind."

"And this is one of those matters, I suppose," she grumbled.

The situation was all too clear to her, despite her incredulity. Her step-father had been misled and now she and her family would be out on their ears. Drat that old Dovington! And drat the new one, too. He was likely no better than his father.

"I'm sure the new earl was thrilled to find that Renford Hall is thriving and at his disposal," she continued her grousing. "It only makes sense that he will now want to pillage what he can from it to save the rest of his destitute estate—never mind that my family and I will be left homeless."

"Your step-father did not leave you penniless, as I recall, Miss Langley. He thought you would have the property, but that was not all he left behind, was it?"

"No, of course it was not. He did all in his power to see that we were cared for."

"Yes, he was a good man. Mr. Renford left more than sufficient funds for you, your mother and your sister to live on quite comfortably."

"Indeed he did, but that was before I knew we'd have to live on it somewhere else, Mr. Milson. Since my step-father's passing I have used those funds he left us to modernize operations here. I've replaced barns, had all the roofing redone, and built deeper wells for the tenants. I've had extensive improvements made to this house, invested in new farming techniques and put in orchards and irrigation channels. Oh, but Mr. Milson, you simply don't understand. I dropped every last penny of my step-father's money into this house and these lands. If Renford Hall is not ours... well, then I'm afraid Mamma, Ella and I truly have nothing."

"You really have nothing left?"

"Nothing to speak of, Mr. Milson."

"Then I am sorry for you. I wish I had come with better news today."

"As do I," she agreed, rising from her seat and going to stare out the window over the landscape she still thought of as her own. "And to think, I prided myself on being so sensible. I expected to begin recouping our investment this autumn with the promise of excellent harvest and profit from the increased herds and the flocks. I thought I would have more than enough money to pay for Ella's introduction to society next year, just the way my step-father wanted."

'It really is a shame, Miss Milson. I'm sure if he'd had any notion that..."

The man's voice trailed off. Clearly there was nothing he could say to take away the sting of reality. Step-Papa was gone, Mamma was fading, and Ella would not have the Season she'd been looking forward to all of her young life. They'd likely end up in a garret somewhere, barely eking by. Somehow.

But this was not Mr. Milson's burden to bear. Mariah forced a smile and tried to appear hopeful when she pulled her eyes from the scenery and turned back to the matters at hand.

"At least the money Step-Papa put into trust for Ella's dowry is still there. When it comes time for her to marry, she'll have that to recommend her."

But Ella was still only seventeen. She'd not been into the world yet and seemed very much a child. Given their circumstances, it was unlikely the girl would attract any sort of decent suitor for some time—if ever. Until then, Mariah simply couldn't see how they would live.

"And what of you, Miss Langley?" Mr. Milson asked. "Surely you are of an age to consider matrimony. That would solve things then, wouldn't it?"

Mariah hoped the shock did not show on her face. Of course she was of an age—she was five-and-twenty last November. But how could the man suggest such a thing? Unless... perhaps he did not know. She had assumed, since he was managing these legal affairs for them, that he knew of her background. Apparently he did not.

She was not about to educate him just now.

"As you can see, Mr. Milson, Renford Hall is not crawling with marital prospects, neither for my sister nor for myself. I'm afraid we will have to look to something a bit more immediate for rescue, not some mythical gallant bachelor on a white horse."

Mr. Milson nodded. "Well, perhaps the new earl will see your difficulty and agree to share a percentage with you come harvest."

She had to laugh out loud at that thought. They were to sit around and wait for alms from the earl? It was nearly as ridiculous as the suggestion of her marrying.

"You believe the earl will share? I cannot hold such hope, Mr. Milson, given the man's heritage. Surely if his financial affairs are as bad off as you say then he will hardly be interested in sharing any profit from Renford Hall."

"Perhaps things are not as bleak for the man as they were when he first took the title. It's been a year, after all."

One glance at Mr. Milson and she knew he did not believe his own words. No, very clearly he knew only too well how desperate this earl was. Even if the new Dovington was the sort given to charitable actions, it was obvious he stood in no position to be charitable toward them.

"I think you know as well as I do, Mr. Milson, that my family and I can hardly count on help from Lord Dovington."

She would have loved to hear him dispute that, to stand up for the man's character and claim that the new earl was nothing like his dissolute father and would likely help if he could. But he did not. Mr. Milson's silence on the matter told her everything she needed to know about the current Earl of Dovington and his character. Obviously the new earl had none. She supposed she should not be surprised; like father, like son, as they say.

"So this Dovington is no better than his dissipated sire."

She sighed and turned back to the bright landscape outside, still as fresh and as vibrant as if her world had not just come crashing down on her. How on earth was she going to drag herself away from this place? And worse, how was she going to break this awful news to Ella? This was the only home she'd ever known, her last connection to her dear Papa. And Mamma... her health had been waning since losing Step-Papa. To take them both away from Renford Hall was pure cruelty.

"Tell me, then," she asked the solicitor, still gazing at the hills and trees and wishing to memorize every inch of it. "How long do we have?"

"For what, Miss Langley?"

"How long before this degenerate tyrant, Dovington, shows up here to throw us out to the wolves?"

Mr. Milson did not answer. Instead, a low rumble startled her from the doorway. A voice she'd not heard before replied, words sounding more like a growl than actual language and causing her very bones to vibrate inside her.

"Not long at all," the voice said. "The degenerate tyrant, as you say, has arrived."

She spun quickly and was left gaping in horror. The rare April sunshine spilling in through the window suddenly dimmed. The air in the room abruptly went cold. The doorway was filled by a stranger—a man. He was tall and clad all in black, from his elegant neck cloth to his long traveling coat. He'd not removed his hat and it sat at an angle atop his head, waves of nearly-black hair framing an angular face. His eyes were dark but flashed with fire as they latched onto hers.

"Lord Dovington!" Mr. Milson exclaimed, leaping to his feet.

The introduction had not been needed. Mariah knew to her deepest core who this gentleman was the instant his voice reverberated through her. Good heavens, but "tyrant" had been far too mundane a word for him. Perhaps "demi-god" suited him better.

"As for throwing you out to the wolves," the man said, not being the least bit subtle as his animal eyes roved over her, head to toe. "I suppose we shall see how long that will take."

Chapter 2

Dovington had not been in this house for over twenty years, as best he could recall. He knew it well, though. When the footman had opened the door to him and informed him that the solicitor had gone to meet with some Miss Langley person in the study, he'd known just how to find them there.

Over the years he'd learned that showing up places unannounced gave him an advantage, and this case was no different. He'd arrived outside the study just in time to hear a beautiful woman disparaging his character. That was not surprising in itself—it had happened before. What made it unique this time, however, was the fact that he had no idea who she was.

Generally when women disparaged him, they had good reason. This one, however, was an absolute stranger to him. He could only wonder what he had done to gain such an unwarranted—at least so far—opinion from her. From the looks of her, though, he wouldn't mind giving her reason to warrant those opinions. She was just the sort of spirited armful that might make his unpleasant return to this, his childhood home, somewhat endurable.

"I suppose an introduction is in order," he had said, pulling off his gloves and stepping into the room. "I am the Earl of Dovington."

"Yes, that's already been established," the green-eyed spitfire replied.

He had been none too subtle with his perusal of her person and now she returned the favor. She eyed him as if he were the devil himself, walking into her parlor with mud on his boots. Frankly, he could not recall when distain and disapproval had ever looked so damn fetching on a woman.

"Well, then, perhaps you ought to enlighten me as to your identity, miss," he said.

The other gentleman in the room—a solicitor he'd met once on matters regarding this estate but whose name was unimportant to him—blustered toward them.

"My lord, this is—"

He raised up his hand to shush the fellow. "No. Let her tell me."

Her eyes went large. Good. He'd offended her. That put her at the disadvantage.

"Very well, I shall introduce myself, sir," she said. "I am Mariah Langley."

"Yes, so I was told at the door. But who *are* you? What is your position in this house?"

"My position, sir?"

Damn it, but she'd seemed much more clever than this. He hated being disappointed this early in his acquaintance with an otherwise desirable female.

"Yes, your position. I'm told the leaseholder was a fellow named Renford. You are Miss Langley, so you cannot be his wife nor his daughter. What are you then? His mistress, perhaps?"

"Certainly not!" she exclaimed. "Mr. Renford was my step-father, sir."

He shrugged. "Doesn't entirely rule out the suggestion of mistress..."

She did not rise to his bait. Instead of swooning or going pale at his bold insinuation, she simply glared at him. One elegant eyebrow cocked as if she were above even acknowledging such lewd conversation. The eyebrow itself indicated that she did acknowledge it and did not find it humorous.

"Why are you here, sir?" she said with complete composure. "Come to merely inspect your estate, or to throw helpless women out into the street?"

Now he had to smile at her. Indeed, his first impression had been accurate. She was both feisty and clever, a potentially dangerous combination. Added to that the fact that she had all her teeth, a most excellent complexion, and the finest bosoms he'd seen outside of London meant he was going to have to tread carefully here. This was a game he dared not lose, but at the same time he was determined to enjoy.

"I've not met the other female members of this household, Miss Langley, but I daresay you would never be counted in any collection of helpless women."

"I would prefer not to be counted in any collection of women at all, sir. We are not collectibles. But I would very much like an answer to my question."

"I daresay it hardly matters what my intent was upon arriving here," he said, impressed that her green eyes met his without hesitation. "You would be a very difficult woman to throw out of any place, Miss Langley."

He could easily think of a few places he might like to throw her *into*, of course. Not that he would mention them to her just now. Boudoirs and beds were likely off limits for discussion, as far as she was concerned.

"I do not worry for myself, sir, but for my mother and sister," she said stiffly.

"Ah, Mrs. and Miss Renford. But surely they have family they can go to?"

"My step-father did not have many connections, sir."

"But what of you, then? Surely there are other Langley's you can turn to. Where are your father's people?"

"I know nothing of them, sir. Langley was my mother's name and her people have been estranged to her for... well, since several months before I was born."

There was only one thing Dovington could make of that statement. The fine-bosomed spitfire was a bastard. Yet here she stood, facing him with her pretty chin stuck up in the air as if she were a royal duchess. How peculiar. And how compelling. She presented herself very much the lady of quality, yet when asked she had looked him in the eye and announced she was not. A very interesting woman, indeed. He should enjoy finding out more about her.

So he could use her to his advantage, of course. What

became of this chit or her family once he took full possession of the estate was none of his concern. He could not afford to worry over them; he had more than enough of his own worries, thanks to his damnable father and the mess he'd made of what had once been a proud and powerful title.

Also thanks to that damnable man, Dovington was well versed in the fine art of using people for his own purposes. He'd had to learn that to survive. Fortunately, he could also thank the man for being heartless and cruel. That meant he'd had none of those useless traits like guilt and compassion to pass on to his son. The current earl could be ruthless and cold and never worry about feeling any remorse for his behavior.

Why should he? After all, he was his father's son. No one expected any better of him than that.

Clearly the solicitor did not. He was clearing his throat and turning his hat nervously in his hands as he approached the earl.

"You must understand Miss Langley's situation," the man began. "It came as a great shock to her that the property was not held in fee simple by her step-father. When the transaction was made years ago, your father led him to believe the property was not in entail and that it could be sold to him outright."

"Obviously my father lied," the earl said.

His honesty seemed to startle the man. He'd found most people reacted that way when confronted with a harsh truth that would usually be sugar-coated or skirted around. But Dovington never coated *nor* skirted. That was both a waste of time and a waste of a perfectly good opportunity to maintain the upper hand in a situation.

"My father was a liar, pure and simple," he continued, pleased with the look of discomfort and confusion over the solicitor's face. "He squandered his fortune and then cheated and lied to whomever it pleased him in an effort to get his hands on more money to squander. I make no apologies for him."

"Then you are willing to come to a solution that will satisfy Miss Langley?"

"Indeed, I would be most willing to satisfy Miss Langley," Dovington said, giving her a smile she could in no way misunderstand. "She will be happy to know I can satisfy her here for a full three days before she and her family need to vacate this home."

Susan Gee Heino

Chapter 3

The man was a beast—a huge, terrifying, beautiful beast. Not that she would ever be attracted to his brand of dangerous magnetism. Let him leer at her as he did; let him rake over her person with those dark, archangel eyes. Other women might be tempted by his aura of power and the dangerous passion that virtually oozed from him. She was not.

Nor would she be intimidated, even if she felt a bit like a mouse staring into the gaping maw of a ravenous lion. This was her home, her family's home. The law of the land might be on his side, but the fact was that she was here and it would take more than some dark-eyed posturing on his part to remove her. At the very least, it would take more than three days.

No matter what he insinuated he might plan on doing for those three days, the randy letch.

"Sorry to inconvenience you, my lord, but there is absolutely nothing you could say—or do—that would give me any satisfaction at all in just three day's time," she said, making sure by her tone that he knew she understood him full well and was not amused. "I'm afraid three days is hardly time to make arrangements for my family to be removed elsewhere. I advise you to return to wherever it is you came from and we will see that you are notified when our plans have been settled."

If she had been hoping to set him off guard by her defiance—a thing she was certain he was unused to seeing—she was left disappointed. The fire in his eyes merely burned hotter and the corner of his elegant lips twisted into an interested half smile. Apparently all she'd achieved was to lay down a challenge before him. Drat. That was the last thing she needed.

"You would be amazed what might be accomplished in three

days time, Miss Langley. I can be most... persuasive."

"Some things cannot be persuaded, sir. Furniture, for instance. I doubt even you could persuade all of our things to get up and make their way to some new abode—even if we had some new abode to send them to. I'm sorry, sir, but the process will take considerable time."

"Three days, Miss Langley. That is all the time you have."

"Oh? And what will happen at the end of those three days? The house will vanish in a puff of pixie dust? Barbarians will arrive at the door to begin pillaging and plundering?"

Clearly he was equally unamused by her tone. "No. Not pixies or barbarians, I'm afraid. It's much worse."

"Worse? What could possibly be worse than barbarians?"

"Americans."

"Americans?"

"Yes. Americans with money—the worst kind."

"You are serious?"

"I am," he said as if pronouncing sentence on all of them. "I am negotiating to let this house. In three days time the Vandenhoffs of New York will be arriving here to stay for a week to decide whether or not they wish to make residence here for the duration of summer."

"You have leased our house already?" She could barely stammer the words out for all the choking anger she felt. "While we are still living here?"

"No, by the time they arrive you will no longer be living here. The house will be vacant."

"It most certainly will not be!"

"It had better be, Miss Langley. You cannot very well expect me to offer them a house that is already full, can you?"

"But three days, sir... impossible. It simply cannot be done."

"Of course it is possible, Miss Langley. This is my house and I am giving you three full days to vacate it. Perhaps you'd best stop whining now and get on with your preparations."

Her body wanted to crumble into a weepy, broken pile on the floor but she willed herself to stand firm. Lord Dovington was frightful in his demands, moving toward her as he spoke so that now he loomed large. He glared at her, the air around him sizzling as if something dreadful would happen if she so much as thought of disobeying his command.

But what choice did she have? There was no way they could have a whole lifetime removed from this house in just three days, even if she wanted to. The man was being completely unrealistic and cruel. She hated cruelty even more than she feared the burning menace smoldering in Dovington's dark eyes.

"No."

"What was that?"

"I said no, my lord."

"I thought that's what you said. What on earth does it mean?"

She could well understand the man had not often heard the word, but she doubted he truly did not know it's meaning. She'd be happy to remind him of it, though. Often.

"It means you cannot come barging in here demanding your way, sir. It means I have no intention of making any preparations whatsoever. It means this is our home, and my family and I are not leaving any time soon." She could see the fury building behind his hard expression, yet she hesitated only a little before delivering her final blow. "Certainly not before, as you say, you have satisfied me."

That clearly caught his attention just as much as her "no" had. The arrogant bounder.

"Now you're talking sense," he said with a half-smile every bit as blistering as it was cold. "And just what sort of satisfaction have you in mind, Miss Langley?"

"I'm talking about payment of what you owe us for the twenty-years my family managed your property," she replied, keeping her voice icy and tight. "I'm sure Mr. Milson will be happy to help me figure out what these numbers must be and then draw up the papers. Once you have paid that debt, sir, I will be satisfied. My family and I will gladly leave Renford Hall."

He steamed at her. "It's *The Grove*, damn it. This house has been called *The Grove* since my great-grandfather started building it in 1690."

"Well it was renamed *Renford Hall* when your derelict father fraudulently sold it to William Renford a hundred-and-some years later and I'll thank you to watch your tongue, please."

She could see him struggle to regain his temper, but he did so. His fists tightened and he took a deep breath or two, but eventually he calmed and inclined his head toward her.

"Forgive me. I concede this situation must be as uncomfortable for you as it is for me but let us agree on one thing: the Americans are coming and a solution must be reached before they arrive. I have no way to contact them as they travel, and I can hardly slam the door in their faces when they arrive. Mr. Vandenhoff is highly regarded in his native land. Would you have him haul his wife and daughter off to some lowly inn for a week while you and I argue over details?"

She hardly felt twenty years of investment into this home and the notion of her family out on the street were details, but one thing in his lordship's words did catch her ear.

"They have a daughter?"

"Yes. Miss Mable Vandenhoff on her first voyage abroad."

"So she is not a child, I take it."

"Nineteen, I believe."

Ah, now things were becoming clear.

"And she is an heiress, I presume?"

"Her father is quite wealthy and she is his only child so yes, it is safe to call her an heiress."

She'd heard rumors of these sorts of Americans. Men who through their own sweat and their cunning amassed great fortunes from shipping or finance or God-only-knew what. Perhaps they had even found a way to profit from the recent wars between their two nations. But now that the wars were over and the world had fallen, more or less, into peace, it was not uncommon for ambitious Americans to seek to better themselves through attachment with their former enemies. Specifically, they invaded England hoping to marry their daughters off to penniless peers in exchange for some pretense of nobility.

And Lord Dovington fit that description most perfectly.

So this was the reason he was so eager to play host to these Vandenhoff's. He must realize the only way to save his estate would be to marry well, and soon. On one hand, this obviously meant Mariah's hopes were thin for getting the man to pay them what he owed for all the investment she'd put into Renford Hall:

he was obviously as desperate as she feared. On the other hand, though, it meant that if she helped the odious man marry that heiress, he'd have ample funds to pay her.

And more, if he married their daughter, Mr. and Mrs. Vandenhoff would probably wish to make their English home elsewhere—most likely they'd want to be nearer their daughter and her husband at the main Dovington estate all the way up in Surrey. They would not wish to lease this home, certainly. If the man were happily wed and his pockets newly filled, Mariah might even be able to negotiate another lease on the Hall. She and her family could stay. It would be the answer to their prayers!

All she had to do was make sure this visit from the Vandenhoffs went well and ended productively.

"I believe I know the solution, sir," she said giving him a sweet smile. "My mother, as lady of this house, would love to play hostess to your American friends. We would be honored to have them as guests here."

He did not seem to know what to make of her words and clearly did not trust her.

"The goal, Miss Langley, is that at the end of the week they will determine they wish to make this house their residence. They are not looking to be indefinite houseguests."

"Of course not. But as I told you quite plainly, there is simply no way my family and I can be out of here in three days time. If we acted as hosts, however, that would not put the Vandenhoffs in any sort of awkward position while they peruse the house, and my family and I will have time to see about making other arrangements."

He was hesitant to acknowledge the obvious brilliance of her suggestion.

"You will not use that opportunity to set the Vandenhoffs against letting the house?"

"I am not petty, sir," she replied, miffed. "I will not leave the house within three days, but I am no fool. I know the law leaves me little recourse. You own this house and my family does not. You say we must leave and I have no way to argue. I believe, however, that taking these extra days to play hostess to the

Vandenhoffs will give my family the time we need to actually comply with your wishes. As for *my* wishes, these extra days will allow you and me to come to terms on that matter of repayment."

"I see."

"You will be staying here along with the Americans, I presume?"

He frowned. "Yes, I suppose I must. Very well, Miss Langley. I concede your plan holds some merit. It seems this will be the best solution—however temporary—for all of us."

"Thank you, sir. It is good to see that you can be reasonable—however temporary."

Now there was only heat, no ice, in the grin he gave her.

"Funny, Miss Langley, but I was just thinking the same thing about you."

Chapter 4

Lord Dovington paused in the doorway of the elegantly decorated bedroom the servant had led him too. Miss Langley had still been fuming when she politely invited his lordship to leave the office and make himself more comfortable upstairs. She'd called for the housekeeper and not given Dovington time to decline. He was dismissed from her presence after she'd made him agree to her terms.

Lord, but what a head-strong, insolent woman. When he'd first surprised her by walking in unannounced he'd mistaken her wide, dewy eyes as harboring fear; he'd seen her pretty sprigged gown as just frills on a decorative bauble; he'd thought her feminine form as just something pleasing for his eyes as he managed this situation. How wrong he'd been, though!

Miss Langley was far from the simpering, pampered miss he'd expected. She was a formidable force and he'd not take that for granted again. She'd played her hand well and won in this round. While Dovington had to admit to himself he'd enjoyed every minute of it, he could not let her keep pressing him into a corner. He couldn't worry what would come of her, either.

The servant had lead him up the grand staircase, but at the top of the landing they had turned to the left while instinct had tried to send him the other way. To the right had been the wing of the house reserved for family. To the left were the rooms used by guests. This was where he should be right now, despite how odd it might feel.

Oh, certainly this room before him now was well-aired and as comfortable as he could hope for, but it was a guest room. Very likely he'd never been in this room before, and certainly he d never slept in it. It felt as foreign to him as if... well, as if he

23

truly were a stranger here.

Which he was, after all. Despite the fact that his own ancestors had built the house, he was nothing more than an unwanted guest now, even though he owned the place and had played in these halls as a carefree young lad. Well, perhaps not as carefree as lads ought to be, but he did still hold some pleasant memories of this house.

As did Miss Langley, he reminded himself. She couldn't have been much more than an infant herself when she came to live here. He'd best remember that and tread lightly as he proceeded. The woman clearly viewed this as her home.

Which would work to his advantage, he realized. No doubt she resented him completely, yet the Vandenhoff family would be arriving soon and he doubted she'd wish to be seen as anything less than an excellent hostess. She took her role here quite seriously and she would surely put some effort into making the American's feel welcome. That was exactly what Dovington wanted.

If Tobias Vandenhoff liked what he found here at The Grove—or Renford Hall, as he supposed Miss Langley would stubbornly refer to it—he and his family would stay. If they stayed, then Dovington's plan stood a ghost of a chance. That American fortune would find its way into Dovington's coffers and the whole estate—as well as his name—might yet be saved.

Miss Mable Vandenhoff was eager to find herself an aristocratic husband, or so her father assured him. What better place for her to find such a candidate than at a gracious country estate during a pleasant house party? Miss Langley would be the unwitting matchmaker that would save the Dovington line. Pity that she'd have to give up her home in the process, but he refused to let himself be sentimental. He had his duty to perform and no silly emotion or petty concern could get in the way of that.

"He's not throwing us out, Mamma," Mariah carefully explained for the hundredth time. "But unfortunately, it is his house and he has every legal right to do so."

"Dear William bought the house! He bought it for me, when

we married," Mamma moaned, shaking her head and dabbing her eyes with a crumpled handkerchief.

"I know, Mamma. Step-Papa did everything just right and gave us a lovely home. It was not his fault the old earl cheated him this way."

Clearly the shock of it all was taking a heavy toll on Mamma. Drat that infernal earl for showing up this way and making things far more difficult than they needed to be. Mamma simply couldn't take this sort of strain on her delicate sensibilities. It was as if she were losing her dear husband all over again. Three years he'd been gone and still Mamma was not out of mourning. She'd lost so much of her spark that Mariah worried she'd never get it back. And now this... How was the poor woman to endure?

"But where will we go?" Her younger sister paused for a moment from her anxious pacing to perch nervously on the edge of the sofa, batting huge blue eyes and waiting for an answer that might give her some kind of reassurance that all would be well.

"We will stay here. At least for now," Mariah confirmed. "I have managed a bargain with the earl."

Mamma was clearly dubious of that. "A *bargain*? We've all heard what sort of man the Earl of Dovington is. What sort of bargain could you possibly reach with him?"

"Nothing to worry about. He needs a hostess, Mamma," Mariah went on quickly and hoped she sounded at least a little bit positive about their situation. She would need Mamma and Ella's cooperation through this if she had any dream of it working. "I told him you would be happy to play that role."

"What? You told him that *I*...? Good heavens, Mariah. What can you possibly mean?"

"I mean the earl is expecting guests. Here, at Renford Hall. We are either to vacate the house, or stay and make his guests welcome."

She hadn't intended on being quite so blunt with Mamma, but there simply was not time to treat the matter softly and gently. She needed Mamma to understand the importance of this and she needed her help.

"Please, Mamma. I know it is an insult to require this of you

25

here in your own home, to be gracious to strangers and dance to this man's bidding, but I believe it is the best thing for us."

"How can you say that, Mariah? Your father is in his grave and we are being evicted from our home. This earl demands that I play hostess to some of his degenerate friends and you tell me it is for the best? No, I cannot see how."

"But it is, Mamma. These friends of the earl's, they are American. Moreover, they are wealthy and have a marriageable daughter."

"What is that to me? I have two marriageable daughters and I daresay it will do neither of your reputations any good at all to be seen hosting friends of that rogue."

"The earl intends to marry the American daughter."

"All the more reason we should have nothing to do with her."

"But Mamma, don't you see? The earl has little to recommend him to this heiress. Renford Hall is the jewel in his crown, that has to be why he intends to court her *here*. But surely he has no wish to make this his seat. After all, everyone knows the estate he holds in Surrey is much grander—or could be if the man had any money for it—and much nearer to London. He simply needs to attach the heiress, then they will no doubt remove themselves to Dovington Downs to restore it to glory. They will then be content to let us remain here as tenants. We can go on just as we have been."

"As tenants? In our own home? It's unthinkable."

"You would have us leave, then?"

"I would have this new earl go to the—"

"Mamma, please. We must keep a cool head over this."

"How can I? This is the best bargain you could make with the man?"

"I'm afraid so, Mamma. He is a hard man, but you must believe that if we manage ourselves, this will work in our favor."

"I cannot see how."

"Trust me. If we can somehow make the earl seem appealing, the heiress will have no reason to question his suitability."

"And they will fall in love and go off to be married!" Ella

chimed in as a dreamy schoolgirl might be expected to chime.

"That is the goal," Mariah said, although for the life of her she could not imagine the earl falling in love with anyone but himself.

Still, stranger things had happened, she supposed. And besides, it was hardly a requisite that the couple fall in love. All they needed was for the heiress not to despise the earl long enough to realize she wanted his title. Surely the concerted efforts of Mariah's very determined household could produce that simple effect.

"So he will marry her and then go off and leave us alone?" Mamma questioned.

'Of course," Mariah assured her. "Why would he not? It's not Renford Hall that he cares about, it's the American's and their money. We must simply facilitate his connection with that."

"And all will be as it was?"

"I believe so, Mamma. The earl will have what he wants, the Americans will gain their entrance to society, and everyone will leave us in peace."

"I will have my proper coming-out, just as Papa promised?" Ella asked after digesting it all.

"Yes, just as he promised," Mariah said.

The clock on the mantle ticked off the seconds as Mamma contemplated their dilemma. What she was contemplating, Mariah wasn't quite sure. Clearly they had but one option and she'd just laid it out plainly. There could be nothing more to decide. Still, she was silent and let her mother come to terms with things.

"Very well," Mamma said at last. "I will allow these Americans into my home. I will play hostess."

"Excellent, Mamma. I'm sure they are lovely people, and how interesting it will be to meet them. I've not met anyone from the colonies, have you?"

"No, I daresay I haven't."

"And this heiress," Ella asked. "Do you suppose she is very nearly my age?"

"Two years older. The earl said she is nineteen," Mariah replied. "Perhaps you will make a fast friend."

27

"I think I might enjoy that. She could tell me of her life in the wilderness. I've read they have bears and other fierce creatures roaming everywhere in America!"

"I doubt Miss Vandenhoff has seen many of them, Ella. She's from New York, and it is quite a large city, I've heard."

"Well, I'm sure there are other fascinating things she can tell me. Yes, Mamma, perhaps this is a good thing, after all. It might be fun to have houseguests here at the Hall."

Mamma was still unconvinced. "And the earl? I suppose he'll be staying here, as well?"

"It would be very difficult for him to court the American if he did not," Mariah said. "But don't worry. I'm sure he will be on his best behavior."

"For him, that might very well not be good enough. I cannot say I am happy to be in this situation, Mariah."

"Nor I, believe me. But unless you would rather pack our things and be out on the street within three days time..."

"Three days!"

"Yes, Mamma. That's when the Americans will arrive."

"Why, we hardly have time to prepare for guests in just three days!"

"We'll be fine Mamma. You will be as charming as ever, our servants are always respectful and attentive, and the house is in perfect order to host a small party. You'll see. Before long, Miss Vandenhoff will be swooning at Lord Dovington's feet."

"In that case, let us hope the brute doesn't trip over her."

Chapter 5

Three days had flown by. Mariah barely had time to catch her breath as she made sure all was in perfect order for their guest's arrival. The one guest they already had—the unwelcome earl—had been very much—and very thankfully—absent. She did not pretend to regret that. The times when he had made himself visible in the house he'd been every bit as unpleasant as he'd seemed on their first meeting.

Clearly she would have her work cut out for her if she was to have Miss Vandenhoff swooning at the man's feet any time soon. She could only hope the young lady was of a docile, moldable nature. When the family had arrived just over an hour ago, Mariah had not been given enough time to formulate any opinion of the girl at all before she took herself up to her room for refreshing. With dinner just minutes away now, Mariah was eager for their American guests' reappearance and an opportunity at last to assess this person who was ultimately pivotal in Mariah's plan.

"Have they come down yet?" Ella asked, poking her head into the drawing room where Mariah waited.

"No, none of them yet."

Ella must have doubted her for she glanced carefully around before actually entering. "Not the earl?"

"No, he's been away all day and I've no idea when he'll turn up."

"Good. I don't like when he's here. He's so stern and so serious all the time. And I don't like how he looks at everything in our house as if he's trying to estimate the value of it."

"He probably is."

"Well, not all of it is his. Some things are ours and we can

29

take them when we go, can't we, Mariah?"

"Of course. I've been drawing a list so there will be no question when it comes time for us to go. *If* it comes time for us to go."

"You really think there is still hope that we might stay?"

She would like to feel a bit more certain of it, but she managed to assure her sister all the same. "Of course there is hope. And now that the Vandenhoff family is here, we are one huge step closer to building that hope."

Ella wrinkled her nose as she plopped gracelessly into the sofa. "I can't imagine anyone wanting to marry that earl, not even an American. He's terrible."

"Hush! Would you have him walk in and hear you?"

Now Ella looked horrified. "My gracious, no! He'd turn those dark, frightful eyes on me and I'd likely melt into the floor. Heavens, are you so sure we ought to wish him on Miss Vandenhoff?"

"He's a titled nobleman so she'd be a countess. That's not something to dismiss lightly, even if the man is somewhat unpleasant. And you must admit, Ella, he is at least pleasant to look at, when he's not glaring or skulking or making demands."

"I don't think I've ever seen him when he's not doing those things." Apparently the mere thought of it caused her to giggle. "Sorry, but I can't think of him as pleasant."

"You don't think so? His features are classically attractive, and even though he does choose to dress as an undertaker, he does so with elegance."

"But he must be all of thirty years old! Poor Miss Vandenhoff, to come all this way from America only to end up married to someone like that."

"Thirty years old is not quite ancient, not for a gentleman," Mariah chided. "I myself will be that age before too very long."

"You are hardly so old. And even when you are, you will not be half as unlikeable as Lord Dovington."

"Well, I should hope not. I shall try not to turn into a withered, grumbling ogre over the next few years."

Ella giggled, but their wicked glee ended up cut short. Once again, Mariah was frozen by that voice from the doorway.

"I'm an ogre now?" he asked. "I suppose that is better than the tyrant I was on my first day here."

The sound of a small mammal having its tail stepped on eeked out of Ella. Mariah, however, was beginning to get used to his lordship's annoying habit of turning up just in time to hear her speak badly of him. She simply stiffened her backbone, turned, and gave him a condescending smile.

"I see you are returned just in time for dinner, my lord," she said. "You'll be happy to hear that our guests have arrived. They should be down presently."

' Excellent. I shall try not to grumble or make my decrepit self particularly ogre-ish for them."

"I'm sure they will appreciate that," Mariah replied, although the look Ella shot her clearly insisted she should have been just a bit more apologetic.

"I trust the family was properly welcomed and has been afforded every element of hospitality?"he said which, by the mere fact that he felt compelled to ask such a thing of her, was every bit as insulting as her words to him.

"Of course, sir. I sent them down to the kitchens with specific instruction they be offered our best gruel and stale bread."

"Mariah, you did not!" Ella gasped. She twisted her fingers together and blinked up at the earl. "She is funning you, sir. I promise, the Vandenhoffs have been given our best rooms and a full complement of servants to look after them."

"Of course, Miss Renford," he replied, somehow managing a nearly charming smile for the girl. "I recognize your sister is simply teasing. No doubt the Vandenhoffs are enjoying their stay here already. But tell me, Miss Langley, what do you think of these Americans? Are they as you expected?"

"I've never met any Americans so I'm afraid I have no expectations, sir," she said in the most civil tones she could locate. "And I'm sure my opinion hardly matters one way or another. I would so much rather hear what you think of them."

"As I've not met them myself I'm afraid I have no judgment to offer. Ah, but I believe I hear them on the stairway now. It seems we will be forming our opinions together."

And she was determined his would be a positive one. Miss Vandenhoff had appeared pleasing enough, if perhaps a bit plain, but no doubt anyone would seem lackluster after such lengthy travel. Mariah would make it her duty to attend to the girl's every need and have her presenting in the best possible light right away.

"Here we are, this is the room," Mamma's voice sang sweetly out in the corridor.

She led the Vandenhoff family into the drawing room. The earl had been filling up most of the empty space, but he stepped aside to allow Mamma and the two Vandenhoff ladies to enter. Mr. Vandenhoff followed behind, a short man whose well-fed belly proceeded him into the room, but whose demeanor had been jovial enough on their brief meeting earlier. He smiled amiably and acknowledged the party inside the room with a nod and a bow.

"I see everyone has assembled," Mrs. Vandenhoff said with her unpolished accent. "I'm sorry if we kept you all waiting."

"Not at all," Mariah replied, then wondered if perhaps it should have been the earl's place to acknowledge them first.

It was, after all, his house. Since he'd never before met his own guests, though, she supposed she was in order. At least as much as any of this could be. She caught Mamma's eye and gave a tiny nod, hopefully reminding her to make proper introductions.

Not used to playing hostess for such unusual company, Mamma seemed momentarily flustered then managed to recall herself. She cleared her throat and turned to face the earl.

"My lord, may I present Mr. Vandenhoff, his lovely wife, and their very charming daughter, Miss Vandenhoff?"

The earl responded exactly as he should have, politely and masterfully. There was hardly any trace of his usual scowl or leering condescension. Mariah was most impressed. So, the horrid man could behave himself, after all. Excellent. That would make her task all the easier.

Obligatory inquiries into everyone's well-being and the course of the Vandenhoffs' recent travel, then at last it was time to go in to dinner. Mariah had fussed nervously over the preparations earlier in the kitchen until cook had finally thrown her out. Of course the meal would be excellent; Mariah had no need to worry. Their servants were more than competent. By now everyone in the household knew how important it was to make a good impression.

Miss Vandenhoff, however, did not seem to be doing her fair part in it. The young lady had been mostly silent until they were all seated in the dining room and the first course was being brought in. As it turned out, turtle soup was apparently not to Miss Vandenhoff's liking.

"It is too strong," she said without ceremony, or without ever tasting her bowl. "I am not one to indulge in rich meals and needless delicacies. A simple broth or a weakened porridge is more than sufficient."

Mariah caught Ella's horrified expression and silently willed her sister to stay silent. Perhaps Miss Vandenhoff was feeling unwell after all their travels, or perhaps this was nothing more than the American way to show gratitude for the excellent meal laid out before her. She simply would not allow herself to assume the girl was being intentionally rude. No, it couldn't be that. All her hopes rested on the supposition that Miss Vandenhoff had innumerable fine qualities and that the earl would notice every one of them.

"Perhaps some bread, Miss Vandenhoff?" Mamma offered, catching the eye of the extra footman they'd hired specifically to help tend to the needs of their guests.

He responded promptly and offered the loaf to Miss Vandenhoff in an elegant manner. She, however, turned up her nose.

"It is written that man shall not live by bread alone," she said stiffly. "As we all know, that includes women, as well."

"Oh, but soup and bread aren't the only courses," Ella piped up quickly. "The remove will be here soon. Stewed eels, I believe."

Mariah cringed as Miss Vandenhoff went painfully ashen. Ella didn't seem to notice this and she rattled on about how cook's eels were the best anyone could ever imagine. It was obvious Miss Vandenhoff had no inclination to confirm this for herself.

Drat the girl! How on earth was Mariah going to recommend her to the world-wise earl if she could not find anything to catch her attention in some positive manner? Mariah switched conversation from food onto the scenery the Vandenhoffs must have passed through on their way. Mrs. Vandenhoff spoke in glowing terms of the picturesque cottages and tidy lanes, while Mr. Vandenhoff expressed admiration for the rich farmland around them. Miss Vandenhoff, however, commented merely that the flowers they had passed on the roadside seemed to agitate her allergies.

Oh, but the girl was becoming insufferable. Try as she might, Mariah found herself less and less able to account Miss Vandenhoff's unpleasant demeanor to travel fatigue. She could not credit it to the girl being American, either, as her parents were truly quite agreeable. Miss Vandenhoff, it would seem, was positively determined to be tedious and bland, if not openly rude altogether. It was as if she were a dark cloud hanging over their dinner and Mariah was helpless to do anything about it.

The earl certainly noticed it, too. More than once she caught him rolling his eyes. Oh, he tried not to let his annoyance show, and it was a wonder Mariah had detected it considering he was such a disagreeable sort himself, but clearly he was not thrilled with the young lady's conduct. Mariah would have quite a task ahead of her to bring these two together.

Heavens, given the worried look on Mamma's face and the irritated scowl on Ella's, Mariah would have quite a task ahead of her just getting through dinner tonight.

Chapter 6

Somehow they did survive dinner without anyone saying anything hugely regrettable. Well, anyone besides Miss Vandenhoff. The girl turned her nose up at nearly everything set out before her and when finally Mamma suggested it was time the ladies adjourned to the drawing room Ella nearly leapt to her feet and ran from the table. Mariah could only hope now that the meal was over Miss Vandenhoff might possibly find something—anything—positive to say.

She nearly groaned out loud when Mamma graciously invited the girl to find yet more things to complain about.

"So, Miss Vandenhoff, how do you find your room here? We hope you are comfortable."

Thankfully, Miss Vandenhoff seemed to have run out of grievances. "It was quite adequate, ma'am. I look forward to passing my time there during our stay."

Ella was noticeably brighter at that. "Oh? You plan to spend much of your time up in your room?"

Mariah shot her sister a disapproving glare. "I'm sure Miss Vandenhoff didn't mean to imply she will spend very much of her time cloistered away."

"Of course not," Mrs. Vandenhoff said, shooting her own disapproving glare at her daughter. "She will be in company with the rest of us whenever possible. Won't you, Mabel?"

"I suppose so," Miss Vandenhoff replied with a not-so-subtle huff. "Whether I wish to or not."

"We'll try not to bore you over much," Ella said, just a teensy bit too sweet to sound in any way sincere.

"We do have some lovely shops in the village," Mamma suggested. "Perhaps our girls will entertain themselves there tomorrow. Also, there are many pleasant walks in the area. I do hope both of you find ample ways to amuse yourself during your stay."

Mrs. Vandenhoff seemed honestly appreciative of Mamma's suggestions. Apparently the woman very much approved of the out-of-doors and asked after the walks Mamma had mentioned. Mariah was eager to encourage this hopeful conversation before Miss Vandenhoff had a chance to express further objection.

"Yes, the countryside is very lovely this time of year with everything just coming to life after winter. What sort of activities are you most interested in, Miss Vandenhoff?"

"I enjoy reading," the lady replied, not surprisingly.

Well, it was not following their discussion of out-of-doors activities, but at least it was something the girl seemed to be interested in. Mariah could work with that. She smiled at her.

"How lucky then, as we are all great readers here. My step-father kept a large library."

"Indeed he did!" Mamma chimed in. "We have a good many volumes on travel and gardening and other very interesting subjects."

"We even have a fine collection of the latest novels," Mariah added quickly. "Ella might not admit it, but she spends most every night burning her candles over something gothic and frightful."

"I do not!" Ella exclaimed, then leaned in toward Miss Vandenhoff. "Though I'd be happy to loan you the first volumes of *The Orphan of Tintern Abbey*. The beginning is quite shocking as we find a poor child standing over a man in the agonies of death and—"

Miss Vandenhoff cut her off. "*Improving books*. I only read improving books, Miss Renford."

Ella was clearly taken aback, not to mention disappointed. "Oh. I suppose Papa must have had some of those on his shelves, too."

"No worry. I brought my own."

Ella scowled and was left grumbling under her breath. "Of course you did. How silly of me not to assume so."

Mariah was desperate to find some way to make pleasant

conversation, no matter how obviously contrary the young lady might be. Mamma seemed quite at a loss in the face of such petulance and Mrs. Vandenhoff was clearly embarrassed. What a difficult young lady Miss Vandenhoff was! They all sat in silence for several seconds before Mariah came up with something to say.

"How fortunate that the earl has been able to coordinate his stay here with yours," she said as brightly as possible. "I gather this is the first time you have met him."

"It is," Mrs. Vandenhoff replied. "He and my husband became acquainted through a mutual friend in London. We are honored that he extended this invitation to us."

' He seemed pleased that you could accept."

' You know him quite well, I take it?" Mrs. Vandenhoff asked. "Distant relations, perhaps?"

Drat. She'd not intended to take the conversation around to discuss the earl. She glanced up quickly at Mamma, hoping for help.

"No, er, our connection is not very close.," Mamma replied. "The earl's father and my husband were acquainted some years past, you see. We've only come to know the current Lord Doington more recently."

"Have you not been his tenant all this time?" Mrs. Vandenhoff asked.

The ladies sat comfortably in the nicest drawing room and to any onlooker they would have appeared quite a contented group. However, Mariah could see Mamma's knuckles visibly whiten as she clenched her fists in her lap. The idea of being considered merely a tenant in her own home grated horribly. Of course Mamma could be trusted not to say anything regrettable at the lady's honest mistake, but Mariah glanced quickly toward Ella and made sure the younger girl recognized warning in her eyes. Ella wrinkled her nose, clearly thwarted from speaking out on the subject.

"The earl's father left certain business matters rather disorganized," Mariah explained hastily, with a reassuring smile. "I'm afraid the new earl only recently learned of our existence here."

Mrs. Vandenhoff nodded. "I see. So you are not acquainted well enough with the man to speak to his character."

His character? Oh, sadly Mariah was acquainted well enough to speak quite a lot on the man's character. Unfortunately, she could think of no part of it that might be fit to mention in polite company.

"Mariah knows him best of all of us," Ella said quickly. "She handles Papa's business since he's been gone, so she has been the one dealing with the earl."

"I see," Mrs. Vandenhoff said with narrowed eyes as she studied Mariah. "How very... modern. I did not realize in England it was usual for unmarried ladies to employ themselves in such a manner. You and the earl are often in company, then?"

"I would hardly say that," Mariah replied, quelling the urge to strangle her sister. "I simply assisted our solicitor in his dealings with the earl. I can't really claim to know the man well."

"He's been a guest in your home for some days now, I understand," Miss Vandenhoff persisted. "Surely you *have* come to know him."

"Er, yes, I suppose we have come to know him in some measure."

"And no doubt you've formed a favorable opinion."

What an odd thing for Miss Vandenhoff to assume! Mariah wasn't sure what to make of such a statement, but she hoped it hinted at something promising.

"Have you formed a favorable opinion of him?" she asked the young lady, hoping for missish blushing and other encouragement of infatuation.

She was sadly disappointed.

"I hardly think I can form any sort of opinion at all after merely one dinner," Miss Vandenhoff said with a sigh as if the act of opinion-forming had completely exhausted her. "Although, if I must have one, I say my opinion is that I find the earl overly polite and far too ingratiating for my taste."

Mariah felt her mouth drop open. Were they speaking of the same man? *Overly polite and far too ingratiating?* It was unbelievable. Not only did Mariah know the man to be the exact opposite of those particular things, she could scarcely comprehend that Miss Vandenhoff might find *those* attributes to be something to complain about.

"I'm not sure I understand what you mean," Mariah said.

"I'm sure Mabel simply wishes to have more time to get to know the man," Mrs. Vandenhoff explained quickly. "It was, after all, only one dinner. I hope we'll see much of him in the days to come. Then we can discover all his many finer qualities."

They were hunting the man's finer qualities, were they? She didn't much like the sound of that. While they were hunting, there was no telling what the Americans might discover about him. The earl had been on his best behavior tonight. If even that had not been enough to win over Miss Vandenhoff, how on earth was he going to improve in her eyes under extended scrutiny? The more he was around his prospective fiancée, the more likely he was to show his true colors. Mariah was going to have to do something to help the man.

She decided she might start by cleaning out the collection of newspapers in her step-father's office before any of the Vandenhoff's stumbled upon them. And read them. As she herself had done over the past three days.

Her step-father always had *The Morning Post* mailed to them and even after his death she'd made sure to continue the habit, despite the expense. Usually she found much of the information contained in the pages to be irrelevant to them in their life here in the country, so far from the bustle of London society, but this time it had proven quite educational. She had noticed several references to the Earl of Dovington.

To be truthful, she had intentionally scoured the pages looking for the man's name. She'd not been disappointed. It seemed Society had become very interested in him since he'd gained title. The wags found him specifically notable for two particular reasons: that he was succeeding in restoring his family fortune despite his detractors' predictions to the contrary, and that he did indeed seem destined to succeed in their other predictions. Namely, they predicted that the man might be equally as likely to be shot by a cuckolded husband, deported for insulting the Prince, or mauled by a pack of jealous opera dancers who each one believed he favored her best.

None of those things were likely to recommend him to Miss Vandenhoff. Despite how charming he had made himself appear at dinner—and Mariah was still reeling with surprise over that—there was no denying that he was boorish, self-centered and stubborn beyond reason. It would take every ounce of artifice she possessed to paint him with any other brush.

"I'm sure we will all come to know Lord Dovington better over the next days," Mamma said, distracting the ladies with her sweetness and the flick of her fan. "No doubt he has many finer qualities we will all come to enjoy. He is, after all, an earl."

Excellent point. That was the man's most notable fine quality and, no doubt, what had attracted the Vandenhoffs to him in the first place. Surely Mariah could promote the man by harping on the small matter of his title.

"Indeed, Mamma. Dovington is a very old and admirable title. The earl honors us with his visit."

"Perhaps titles mean something to you," Miss Vandenhoff informed, "but I care nothing for them. A man must be measured by his own merit, not through some accident of birth."

"Now dear, you are not in America," Mrs. Vandenhoff reminded her daughter. "The earl is a highly respected man here. He travels in company with royalty."

Miss Vandenhoff rolled her eyes at that. Mariah was tempted to join her. Perhaps in this one point she and Miss Vandenhoff agreed. The earl *was* a highly respected man, and surely not through any fault of his own. No one knew more about the consequences of this so-called accident of birth than Mariah. A male child born into right and privilege could retain that status no matter how he chose to live his life, while a person born—as Mariah was—under the shadow of disgrace could live as a veritable saint and never quite overcome that stain of origin. It was decidedly unfair.

Mamma must have known how the subject matter affected her, but thankfully, she gave no indication. She continued the conversation brightly.

"Perhaps when the men join us we can ask the earl to tell us about his visits to St. James. I've heard the rooms are exceedingly lovely, and I simply pour over the fashion plates of court gowns. Can you imagine wearing such things?"

"How wonderful it would be!" Ella mused. "When the earl marries, his wife will be presented at court, you know."

If that had been an attempt to further entice Miss Vandenhoff into a favorable impression of the man, it did not seem to have worked. Clearly presentation before sovereigns of some foreign nation did not excite her in the least. Her lip visibly curled.

"No wonder he has not yet found some woman willing to marry him."

"From what the papers say, there are scores of women ready to throw themselves at his feet," Mariah informed her.

As she should have expected, though, that did not have the desired effect, either.

"That hardly serves to recommend the man. Honestly, you may revere his grand title, but I say it makes him puffed-up and overly stiff."

By heavens, the girl's peevishness was beginning to really irk.

"I thought you said he was overly-polite and far too ingratiating?" Mariah snapped.

"Those are clearly affectations to cover his obvious character flaws."

"He's more agreeable than you give him credit," Mariah retorted with a passion that actually sounded as if she believed it to be true.

As all four of the other ladies now regarded her with raised eyebrows, she realized she was every bit as surprised by her outburst as they. *Agreeable*? Had she just declared the pompous, domineering earl to be *agreeable*? Ridiculous. With all eyes on her and their future at stake, though, she was duty bound to defend her position.

"That is, by all accounts he has dealt fairly in business and is properly devoted to managing his estate and looking after his assets."

There. That was at least truthful. The earl had shown himself to be exceedingly devoted to looking after his assets. *And anyone else's assets, too*, if the gossips were to be believed. Particularly assets of the feminine kind.

"It hardly speaks well of a man that he devotes himself to his assets," Miss Vandenhoff said.

"I believe Miss Langley's point was that he is known for dealing fairly in business," the girl's mother said with a patience that bordered on the miraculous. "Fairness is a quality to be admired. It is good to hear that of him."

"I'm sure there are a great many admirable qualities in the earl," Mamma added. "Perhaps as Miss Vandenhoff gets to know him—and as all of us do—we will see him with convivial eyes."

"Mariah already does," Ella piped up. "I didn't notice at first, but as she pointed out a few days ago, he is at least pleasant to look at. When he smiles, at any rate, like he did tonight at dinner."

And again all eyes were on Mariah. Poor, dear Ella. She simply didn't know when to stay silent, did she? And Mariah's cheeks, drat them, did not know when not to flame red. She would have given anything to have a reasonable excuse to go running from the room just now.

Fortunately, Miss Vandenhoff managed to get everyone's attention back onto herself.

"I didn't notice anything pleasant about the man's appearance," she announced. "He's far too tall and I cannot abide such thick, unruly hair. Not that I wasted time looking at him, of course."

Miss Vandenhoff's words made no sense. She thought the man was too tall and his waves of dark hair too thick? There could only be one explanation. No wonder Miss Vandenhoff was so difficult and rude: *she was obviously a lunatic.*

It would have to be a very addled female, indeed, who could possibly not notice the chiseled line of his lordship's classical jaw, the knowing turn of his sculpted lips, the breadth of his shoulders under the elegant cut of his coat. And his eyes! Heavens, one would very nearly have to be dead—or at least have no sight of their own—to overlook the tantalizing fire that burned steadily behind his midnight dark eyes. Poor Miss Vandenhoff must have left her faculties behind in America if she were truly oblivious to all that.

Lord Dovington might have any number of things wrong with him, but none of them had anything whatsoever to do with his appearance.

"Please, Mabel," her mother scolded. "Have a care what you say."

"If you'd prefer I keep my opinions to myself, Mother, I will quite gladly do so."

The girl's impudence was insufferable. Mariah was quite shocked at it, actually. Poor Mrs. Vandenhoff seemed dreadfully uncomfortable as she could do little more here in this public setting than to beg her daughter to behave.

"Of course I value your opinion, my dear. But we are guests here. Isn't there anything that could make you feel more charitable toward his lordship?"

"Perhaps she would like me to ask him to arrive for dinner tomorrow night six inches shorter and balding," Mariah grumbled. "Though I've no idea what we can do about the fact that he's puffed-up and overly stiff."

Mamma's face went ashen and Ellen gasped in horror as the words left Mariah's lips. Neither of them, however, were looking at her. No, their gaze went beyond her, toward the doorway of their comfortable drawing room.

Mariah knew—of course—that his lordship was standing there.

Susan Gee Heino

Chapter 7

Dovington hesitated in the doorway. My, but Miss Langley could turn a phrase. He supposed it was unfortunate that most of her best phrases seemed to be aimed at belittling him, but truly he didn't entirely mind. The look of astonishment and horror he'd read on her expression when she realized he'd overheard—twice now—had proven to be quite priceless.

Once again, she did not let him down. Slowly, she turned to face him and the pink flush of her rosy cheeks first drained away, then flared to a raging blush that made her appear more the impulsive schoolgirl than the laced-up spinster he knew her to be. At least, that seemed to be what she wished for him to believe about her.

These periodic outbursts indicated her lacing might not be quite as tight as she might give impression. She had chinks in her armor of self-control that he found amply entertaining, and enticing. Her reckless insults gave him a glimpse of a woman of strong will, but of strong passions, as well. The best thing about Miss Langley's unbridled tongue, however, was the fact that her careless words continued to place her at his mercy.

"I'm sorry, were you not expecting us to join you?" he asked.

"Er, but of course," she stammered, taking on the role of hostess as clearly her stunned mother was suddenly speechless. "Come in, gentlemen."

Mr. Vandenhoff had come up behind Dovington, his waddling gait keeping him several steps behind so that he had not been privy to Miss Langley's tirade. He appeared not to notice the obvious agitation of the women just now, either. It seemed they were upset by more than just Miss Langley's sharp words regarding her guest. What other interesting discussion had he missed here?

"Your cook is to be commended for that excellent meal," the earl said, finding a place where he could prop an elbow against the mantle and preside over the others in the room.

"Yes, it was most excellent, indeed," Mr. Vandenhoff said. "My family and I have been enjoying trying the new dishes we are discovering on our stay in your country."

Mrs. Vandenhoff agreed with her husband whole heartedly, but Miss Vandenhoff made a noise something akin to a snort. It was not what anyone would call attractive. In fact, very little about Miss Vandenhoff was what anyone would call attractive.

Not that the girl had unpleasant features, exactly, but she simply failed to use them to any advantage. She seemed surly and ready to fight at the least opportunity. Her version of willful defiance was not nearly so engaging as Miss Langley's. No, while the earl found himself eager to step into the fray offered by Miss Langley's sharp words and flashing glances, he wanted to do nothing more with Miss Vandenhoff than hand her over to her father and suggest a good spanking might be in order.

That did not bode well for his plans. Not well indeed. He needed to get his mind off the challenged posed by Miss Langley and get it back on a more productive task. He needed to find some way to make Miss Vandenhoff suddenly blossom into a charming, desirable creature.

That seeming impossibility made his head spin. Surely it would be a much more productive task to amuse himself with Miss Langley. She could do nothing to bring him closer to his goal, but she certainly could make his efforts in the meanwhile less dismal.

Then again, perhaps she could play a more useful role, after all. Dovington would keep his eyes open for just the right opportunity. Any opportunity.

The air of tension in the room lessened some as the conversation flitted from polite discussion about the English diet to trends in American dining and somehow from there onto a little dog Mrs. Vandenhoff once had and was now contemplating getting another. For some reason she wanted Dovington's opinion on the matter and he replied simply that if she wanted a dog, she ought to get herself a dog.

"So you are a dog lover, are you?" the woman asked.

"I suppose that is the term for it," he replied. "My father was very much against keeping pets when I was a child but after we... that is, my mother and I lived for a time at my grandfather's home and I was allowed several dogs there."

"So you must keep hounds at your estate," Mr. Vandenhoff said. "I've heard that is very much the thing with your set."

Yes, Dovington had heard that, too. "No, I'm afraid I have no dogs at Dovington Downs. I've been too caught up with business of late and feel it would be irresponsible to keep dogs that I have no time to exercise or entertain."

Or funds to put the kennels in proper order or supply food of the quality needed to sustain healthy hounds. Someday he would, though. Someday he'd make that damned estate into a *home*. The way Renford Hall had been before... well, the way he liked to imagine it had once been.

"I don't know that I would like keeping hounds," Mrs. Vandenhoff said. "It would be most inconvenient for living in Town. I should like another pug, I believe."

And so the conversation went back onto that. Should she get herself a pug or should she not? Mr. Vandenhoff complained that the last thing their household needed was another body snoring through the night, as pugs were apparently wont to do, and he seemed to think what his wife needed was a loyal, regal spaniel. The other ladies were drawn into the conversation to give their opinions on the matter and this subject occupied them all for a surprisingly long time.

Dovington began to wonder if he'd have any further chance this evening to watch Miss Langley's eyes spark with defiance. Could he provoke that willful tongue of hers yet again? What other interesting things was that tongue capable of?. It seemed pleasant conversation was all he could get out of her right now and he was finding that deadly dull. The whole group of them were boring him to insensibility and all he could think of was finding a way to get Miss Langley alone.

"But if not a pug, I can't imagine what other type of dog I should have," Mrs. Vandenhoff was saying.

Susan Gee Heino

"We visited Bath several years ago and met a lady there who kept a nice dog," Miss Renford chirped brightly. "It was quite small with very lovely white hair. She called him Percy and he was perfect for a lady's companion, I thought."

"And what sort of dog was he? Pomeranian, perhaps?"

Miss Renford shook her head. "I don't know. Mamma, do you recall it?"

"Yes, such a lovable little thing. I don't know what it was, though. I'm sorry."

"A Maltese, I believe," Miss Langley announced. "He was terribly sweet. Ella begged for weeks after to get one of her own."

"And I never did get one," the younger girl said, giving a faux pout. "I'm still very upset."

"He sounds delightful. I've never heard of the breed," Mrs. Vandenhoff said.

"We have a picture of one," Miss Renford declared, then frowned. "At least, we did. Whatever happened to that book, Mariah? You know, the one Papa bought us."

"In the library, I believe," Miss Langley replied. "Remember how we had to keep it up on the top shelf when our neighbor Mrs. Carroll and her small children were here?"

Miss Renford nodded. "That's right, I'd forgotten. Her littlest one was determined to tear out pages and keep them for himself. The engravings are really quite lifelike."

Mrs. Vandenhoff leaned in toward her surly daughter and patted her knee. "Did you hear that, Mabel? You are very fond of dogs. We'll have to spend some time in the library during our stay here."

Miss Vandenhoff was less than enthusiastic, but Mrs. Renford and her daughters appeared fairly ecstatic to find something humane about the girl.

"Perhaps we would all like to see the book," Mrs. Renford suggested. "Mariah, why don't you see if you can go find it and bring it in here?"

Miss Langley nearly leaped up at the opportunity to escape the party, at least for a moment.

"Of course, Mamma. I'll get it right now."

"I'll help you," Dovington said with equal enthusiasm. "As it's up on the top shelf, and all."

Miss Langley pauses, and slid him a glance. She seemed slightly confused and for a moment he caught the hint of worry. It was gone immediately, though, and her expression showed nothing more than the usual overly polite smile she reserved especially for him.

"Very well. I suppose if anyone is to topple off the step stool I would rather have it be you than me."

She spoke the words so sweetly that somehow she managed to make them sound affable. No one in the room realized she was secretly wishing him to break his damn neck. He rewarded her with a smile and a devilish cocked eyebrow he also made sure no one else noticed.

"Or at least I could be there to catch *you* when you topple," he suggested.

Apparently she found that as tantalizingly easy to picture as he did. She blushed in earnest and he felt a distinct sense of accomplishment. Miss Langley presented herself as pristine, yet she understood every one of his innuendos. He was enjoying their game to the fullest.

They left the drawing room and he let her lead the way to the library, as if he could not find the path there in the dark with a blindfold. He was glad for light filling the corridors now, though, so that he could admire the sway of Miss Langley's hips, enjoy the defiant sparks in her eyes when she glanced back to find him admiring.

"The library is here, sir," she said.

"Pity. I was hoping perhaps you had moved it upstairs. Near the bedrooms."

"Sorry to disappoint you, but we use our bedrooms for nothing more than sleeping. This is the area of the house reserved for entertainments."

"Then I'm exceedingly thankful we are here and not there."

She huffed at his impertinence and marched over to a wall of very tall shelving. Pointing with authority, she directed his gaze upward. He let his eyes catch on all her finer qualities as she shifted, of course.

"Up there. That large volume, bound in the burgundy color. That is the book of dog breeds."

"That one?" he nodded upwards in the general direction. "There must be a dozen large volumes on that shelf. Huge, actually. You impress me, Miss Langley. You're clearly quite fond of the over large ones."

"I enjoy reading, sir. Trust me, there is nothing else in this room that could possibly interest me. At all."

He merely shrugged. "Books have their allure, I agree. But you might surprise yourself, Miss Langley, to learn there are other delights between the covers besides reading."

"I think my mother is expecting us to delight our guests waiting in the drawing room with an actual book just now, sir, not some tawdry display of schoolboy bawdiness."

"You're probably right. I can hear Miss Vandenhoff's scathing distain already if I were to suggest anything slightly off-color."

"You'd be put well in your place, that's for certain."

"It's going to take much more than a book to draw any delight out of her, I'm afraid. What do you suppose can be done? Surely you can think of some way to make the girl seem less of a... less..."

He honestly couldn't think of any word to fit there that wouldn't be taken as a direct insult toward the young lady. Miss Vandenhoff was a shrew and a nag of the worst kind, but even he wasn't low enough to go around saying so. Besides, he was hoping for her to be his sister-in-law one of these days. How on earth that would happen, he had no clue. His cousin would likely arrive tomorrow, feel the sting of the chit's sharp tongue, and go running back to his club.

"I'm sure she's simply a bit irritable due to the travel," Miss Langley said. "Surely tomorrow we'll begin to see the softer side of Miss Vandenhoff."

"I certainly hope so. I'd hate for my cousin to arrive and find her out of sorts," he muttered, though he could hardly imagine how else anyone might find the girl.

"Your cousin?"

"Yes. Didn't I mention? My cousin, Edmund Chadburne, is

expected to arrive tomorrow. I'm sure that I told you."

"No. You did not. I would have remembered."

"I was sure that I had."

"You've been too busy pretending I find your insinuations amusing, apparently. You neglected to mention anything of importance, like another guest scheduled to arrive."

"Well, I've told you now. He should be here shortly after noon."

"And is he as charming as you are?"

"Almost. You'll like him."

She rolled her eyes. "I can't wait. Now please bring over the stool and collect the book that we came for."

"I could lift you and hold you until you get what you want," he suggested, purely for his own entertainment.

She stabbed him with her glare. "No thank you. The stepping stool, please."

"Very well," he said, complying and dragging over the stool so he could step up and retrieve the book. "One of these days, Miss Langley, you're bound to let someone come crashing though those barriers you've put up."

"No, your lordship, I assure you that is the last thing that will happen."

He wondered if she realized at that moment she had laid out a challenge it would be impossible for him to ignore.

Susan Gee Heino

Chapter 8

It had been a long, restless night and the morning hadn't gone much better. Mariah was informed a weasel had gotten into the henhouse. They'd lost several good laying hens and two cockerels that had been scheduled for dinner this week. Plus, the most dangerous type of weasel of all had somehow burrowed into Mariah's mind and simply would not leave.

She could not stop thinking about Lord Dovington.

Everything about the man should repulse her. He was vulgar and impertinent. He was stubborn and self-centered. He was the sort of man who would think nothing of ruining a woman's reputation as well as her heart. He was everything she'd devoted her life to avoiding, and here he was, occupying her house and every waking thought.

He interrupted her dreams, as well, and she was furious with herself over that.

What on earth was wrong with her? She knew all too well the consequences of giving in to silly infatuation, to trusting one's heart to a man who should not be trusted with so much as a penny. She knew exactly what sort of man he was *and* that he was destined to marry an heiress he didn't even like simply to gain the girl's money. How could she possibly let the dark promise in his eyes and the teasing grin at his lips be in any way attractive to her?

The man was a tiger, a wild beast. He saw women as nothing more than his next meal. He would single out his prey, happily devour her, ravage her soul, and leave her for dead—metaphorically speaking, of course. But the result would be no less devastating.

Clearly he viewed her as prey. And of course, she would be

the most logical victim here. He knew she had no father, had no claims of respectability. Certainly her step-father had always treated her as his own, but Dovington obviously knew the truth. Ella was a child, the daughter of a gentleman; Mariah was not. Miss Vandenhoff had a doting father and buckets of money; Mariah did not. If Lord Dovington was to amuse himself with any female here, she would be his obvious choice and it had nothing to do with any great merit on her part.

She was merely convenient, and posed no threat in the way of consequences. If he could sway her, he'd be able to take what he wanted then simply walk away without a care in the world. He was the worst sort of bounder and she sensed danger oozing from him.

It was simply abhorrent that her heart would pound and her blood would quicken at the very sight of him. Yet it did. She walked into the breakfast room, simply hoping to make sure the servants had cleared things from earlier, and there he was. Her breath caught in her chest when his eyes fell on her and he gave that dratted, irresistible smile.

"Ah, Miss Langley, we were just discussing you."

Now she noticed a gentleman with him. A few years younger than the earl, this man was not quite as tall, not quite as broad, not quite as elegant, not quite as irresistible, and not the least bit dangerous. The family resemblance was obvious, though. Apparently the cousin had arrived.

"May I present my cousin, Edmund Chadburne," the earl announced as the younger man made gallant show of gushing over his hostess.

"I'm so happy to meet you, Miss Langley," he said in very amiable tones. "Dovey tells me you've done remarkable things with The Grove during your tenure as manager here."

She was impressed to learn that the earl had noticed her efforts, and almost giddy inside to hear that he'd spoken so highly of her. She refused to comment on any of that, though.

"Dovey?"

The earl cringed and his cousin guffawed. "Sorry, *his lordship*, I mean. He hates that old nickname."

"Old nickname? He's only had the title for a year, hasn't he?"

she asked.

"Ah, but he's had the nickname for years. Since school. The coves there saddled him with it because—"

"It hardly matters," the earl interrupted. "As you see, Miss Langley, my cousin has arrived. Your housekeeper was kind enough to lay out an early luncheon for him since he didn't bother to eat along the way."

"It was too nice a day to waste time in a dreary inn somewhere eating bad food. Besides, I couldn't wait to meet... that is, to see my dear old cousin again. He's been so busy working over his ledgers and rolling up his sleeves at that pile of stone there in Surrey that I haven't seen him gallivanting around Town in ages."

"Dovington Downs has needed my attentions far more than London has," the earl said. "But it is good to see you again, Ned. I'm sure Miss Langley and her family will make your visit here quite comfortable."

"Indeed, I hope you feel very welcome here," she said and sincerely meant it even though he did call her home by the wrong name.

"I do, thank you," he replied. "Dovey was just offering to take me about for a look at the lands around here. He says the views are quite good. Why, even just now I was admiring out the window and remarking how very romantic it all is. You have a hermit's hut on the grounds, don't you, Miss Langley?"

She followed his gaze out the window and realized Mr. Chadburne had fixed on the old groundskeeper's hut down past the formal gardens and built into a hillside. Indeed, she hardly paid mind to it herself, but she supposed to a newcomer it must appear somewhat romantic, framed by the green of the hill and two vining roses that were just now going to bud. The most distinctive feature, however, was the red door. It was faded now after years of weathering, but against the backdrop of nature it really was eye-catching.

"We had an old grounds-keeper who lived there, but my step-father built new accommodations for that when I was still just a child."

"I'm sure I see smoke from the pipe, though. Surely someone

lives there," Mr. Chadburne insisted.

"Yes, it is still a snug little house. We have a lodger there right now, someone new to our area who is having a house in the village readied for himself," she explained and hoped the earl wouldn't immediately rush out and raise the poor man's rent fees.

"I see," Mr. Chadburne said with a nod. "It is all even better than expected. I cannot wait to get out and see what other wonders we can find around here."

"We do have many lovely places," Mariah assured him. "The River Itchen flows nearby and you will find ridges and outcrops to provide exceedingly nice vistas."

"Exactly what I need after being pent up in Town for so long. But surely you will join us, Miss Langley?"

"What? Oh, no, I couldn't—"

"Of course you could. Dovey hasn't been here in ages. You must accompany us on our outing so you can point out all the best places to go."

"I'm sure his lordship can find his way without me just fine."

"And what of this Miss Vandinghorfer?" the younger man asked.

"Vandenhoff," the earl corrected. "You must mean Miss Vandenhoff."

"The very one. Didn't you say she is a guest here as well? We'll bring her along, and anyone else Miss Langley thinks we ought to have. We'll make a picnic of it!"

"A picnic? Oh, I don't know that we should—"

"It's an excellent day and what could be more perfect than a picnic out in the verdant embrace of nature? Come, Miss Langley, say you will let us. Everyone longs for the romance of a pleasant day in the countryside?"

Er, no, everyone did not long for that. Romance indeed! She would much prefer never subjecting herself to any situation that could possibly include both Lord Dovington and romance.

Then again, the day was every bit as lovely as Mr. Chadburne said, and Mariah was looking for opportunities to put his lordship together in amiable company with Miss Vandenhoff... yes, perhaps this picnic was what they all needed, after all. She would just take care to ignore any of the inherent romance.

"Very well," she consented. "I'll talk to cook about putting together a hamper for us and find out if others are interested."

"Capital! This is shaping up to be a most distracting holiday for me," Mr. Chadburne said with a grin.

Mariah knew her attempt at a corresponding grin was not nearly so successful. This might be a holiday for Mr. Chadburne, but it was serious business for her. She had to somehow throw together a picnic outing and convince Miss Vandenhoff to come along. Worse, she had to convince the girl to enjoy it.

The earl eyed his cousin once Miss Langley left the room. Ned seemed in high spirits today—a little too high, by his estimation. If his plan was to have any hope of working out, he'd best make very certain his cousin understood his goal here.

"*Verdant embrace of nature?*" he quoted, not holding back on the mocking sneer.

"I thought she might be of a romantic nature and be given to fancy language."

"She isn't."

"She seems a game sort, though," Ned assessed. "And I certainly like the looks of her."

"Well, don't. She's not your quarry and I'll thank you to stop liking her looks or anything about her."

"Oh? Got some designs of your own, cousin?"

The earl snorted at that—perhaps a bit too loudly—but he hoped his quick explanation would cover.

"Hardly. She's my tenant, Ned, and off limits to you. I've brought you here for one purpose and that's what you should concentrate on."

"The heiress. Right. I'll win her over, no doubt, but I don't see why I can't enjoy the rest of the scenery while I'm here."

"Miss Langley is not scenery."

Now Ned was the one who snorted. "She definitely looked like it to me."

"Well stop looking. If you must start making cow's eyes at someone, then Miss Vandenhoff is your aim."

Ned shrugged. "I don't see why you don't just marry her yourself and let me go pick out my own bride."

"We've been over this. I'll put things back to right after my father's embarrassing tenure, but I won't be responsible for future generations. That's to be your purview, I'm afraid, and the Vandenhoff chit is just what is needed to breathe a little fresh air into our bloodline."

"Fresh money, you mean. And my father was nearly as bad as yours was about looking after things," Ned insisted. "I don't see why you're so convinced I need to be the one to carry on the family tree."

"Trust me, your children will thank me."

Ned seemed unimpressed with the prospect. "If you say so. I'm just hoping not to have children who look like the very devil. Is this Vandenhoff chit easy on the eyes? Am I going to have to hide her away in the country all our married life?"

"She's perfectly passable."

"Oh good God. She's a wildebeest, isn't she?"

"Absolutely not. Miss Vandenhoff is adequately sized, has all the right features in all the expected places, and you'll note that her complexion is better than average. She dresses herself well and will be seen as a credit to any man."

"As will her father's money. Are you certain I must go through with this?"

"Yes. The estate needs an heiress, so I've found you one."

"Word around Town is that you've done miracles for the depleted family coffers already. You seem to have a knack for this finance business, Dovey. Why not just keep doing what you have been and let nature take its course? You're putting the estate back to rights, and we can both just go on and marry whomever we please."

"*I* will never marry anyone," Dovington said firmly. "And *you* will marry an heiress; preferably this one. This is the way it needs to be, Ned. Don't tell me you've gone soft in the head and started believing in romantic nonsense about true love and marital bliss. You and I have both seen enough to know that's nothing but rubbish."

"You're right, of course. The Chadburne family hasn't

exactly perfected the art of chivalrous behavior. Still, I can't help but wonder if—"

"Well stop wondering. You're here to attach Miss Vandenhoff. Don't bother yourself with any task but that. Once you've snagged her and produced the obligatory heir, *then* you can go out and start looking for someone to make you happy. Personally, I'd suggest you just find a devoted bulldog instead."

Ned helped himself to another plate of cold meat off the sideboard and shrugged.

"I just don't see why you dislike women so much, Dovey."

"I don't dislike women. I like women very much, as a matter of fact. What I dislike is what Chadburne men become when they attach themselves to women. For you, at least, I have hope that the cycle might be broken."

"I'll do my best for you, old man. You've always been good to us, putting me through school when you were barely out of it yourself, and looking after my Mum and my sisters. I suppose the least I can do is marry this American chit and do right by the family name."

"Well said. Now don't gorge yourself here or you won't have any room for our picnic. I'm sure Miss Vandenhoff won't appreciate having to eat alone today."

Nor would she appreciate dining *al fresco*, or sitting on the ground, or taking sun, or taking chill, or being carried in a litter like a damned Egyptian princess, or any number of things Dovington could imagine. How Miss Langley would manage to get the girl to go along with their plans he had no idea; he only hoped she would accomplish it somehow. Everything hinged on a favorable meeting between the two young people, and Dovington would be damned if he let a little thing like Ned's impulsive request for a picnic ruin his matchmaking plans.

Perhaps he ought to take Miss Langley into his confidence, to convince her how important this was. He could probably find her alone somewhere and hint that easing the way between Ned and the heiress might be in her best interests. Then he could hint at a few other things that might be in her best interests, too.

Chapter 9

"Be sure you take your wrap with you," Mamma was saying as they scurried around gathering the various supplies needed for comfort on their impromptu picnic.

"Yes, mother. I have everything."

"Then why are you frowning?"

"Because it's just that... well, I'm a bit concerned, I suppose."

"About Miss Vandenhoff?" Mamma glanced over her shoulder to make sure no one was nearby as they helped the kitchen staff wrap food for the hamper.

"Yes, how did you know?"

Mamma sighed. "Because I've met Miss Vandenhoff, I'm afraid."

"I just have no idea how to encourage the match between her and the earl. It seems she is eternally contrary. Whatever will cause him to wish to marry her?"

"Oh, I think the man is likely desperate enough to marry even someone like her," Mamma went on in hushed tones. "He'll take her no matter how disagreeable she makes herself. She, on the other hand, is the one you will have to convince."

"By encouraging her to view the earl favorably? I've certainly tried that, Mamma, but I've exhausted the one or two virtues I've been able to detect in the man. For the life of me I can't imagine what could possibly induce either of them to rush into matrimony."

"It is quite the quandary. I fear we will soon need to consider other options. I hold little hope this outing today can produce tender emotions in either one of them."

Poor Mamma. She appeared very down, indeed. Mariah mumbled an encouragement and patted her on her sloping shoulder.

"It will all work out, Mamma" she assured. "It simply has to, right? In the meanwhile, don't worry so much. I'll think of something for them."

But Mamma wasn't reassured. She shook her head and sighed heavily. "I can't help but think it would be good for you to concentrate a bit more on yourself, my dear."

"Myself? Have I overlooked something that needs tending?"

"I mean that you should consider what *you* will do if this scheme to get the earl married doesn't go as we hope."

"I will find us a new place to live. Don't worry, Mamma. If Miss Vandenhoff rejects the earl, I doubt her parents will wish to let the house. Dovington may still try to throw us out of it, but at least we will have some more time."

"Then you should use that time wisely," Mamma advised. "Consider what you might do for yourself."

"I will look after all of us, of course."

"I was thinking you might rather find someone to look after *you*."

"Someone to...? What are you saying, Mamma?"

"I know you've claimed you will never marry, but—"

"Oh, Mamma, you can't be thinking on those lines. Heavens, we'll be making miracles happen to find one decent gentleman to marry Ella when she's out of the schoolroom. To consider finding someone for *me* is... well, it's out of the question."

"No one thinks it's out of the question except you. Mr. Skrewd, for instance, seems to think it is entirely *in* the question."

"Mr. Skrewd? The new curate?"

"Of course. I've seen you with him, you know. He walks with you sometimes, on your way back from the village."

"That's merely for convenience, Mamma, since he's staying in our groundkeeper's hut. Mr. Skrewd is a very nice young man and he's become something of a friend to me, but I assure you there's never been any thought of anything more than that between us."

"We are not so proud that we can look down on a curate, Mariah. He is a relative of the Benson family who hold the living here. Our vicar is not getting any younger, and it stands to reason that Mr. Skrewd will eventually be given the living in his place. You would not live wealthy, but you'd be well cared for and respected as the wife of a vicar."

"Mamma, can you really suggest that? Mr. Skrewd knows of my background. He'd never even consider me."

"He's in want of a wife. You and he get on so well. Why on earth should he not consider you?"

"Because I... because I have no name, Mamma. Please, I know how this upsets you. Let's do not speak of it. The important thing is to focus on getting Miss Vandenhoff to marry Lord Dovington. Then all will be as it should be and if you must daydream about getting one of your daughter's married, you can plan for Ella."

Mamma seemed to want to argue the point, but there were kitchen maids scurrying about and the lack of privacy saved Mariah from having to dwell on the subject. She was happy that sometimes Mamma was able to forget those terrible years in their past when she'd been cast out in shame by her family, when people looked on Mariah with pity and shook their heads, whispering about how sad it was that such a pretty child would never amount to much.

Well, she had amounted to more than enough. She might not truly be a lady, but she was accepted as one here in their little village. She had Mamma and Ella and, by God, she was going to hang onto Renford Hall. Whatever it took, she would see that the earl married his heiress, went back to his ancestral estate, and left them well enough alone here.

"I believe we're ready," she said cheerfully as the last of their things were packed up in hampers. "We couldn't ask for a more perfect day for a picnic. Spring is in the air, and let us hope Cupid's arrows are flying around us."

Mamma made her best effort to smile as she patted Mariah's hand and agreed.

Dovington made sure everything was being loaded properly into the carriages. From the corner of his eye, he watched the house, as well. Where was Miss Langley? Shouldn't she be out here by now, helping see to arrangements? He needed to speak with her and would prefer not to do so with the rest of the group hovering over them.

Ah, there she was, emerging from the house along with two kitchen maids carrying hampers and blankets. Miss Langley seemed perfectly composed as she directed the staff here or there, despite the fact that she must surely feel somewhat put out by Ned's spontaneous demand for a picnic. If the event did not play directly into the earl's scheme he would have shut his cousin down entirely. It was most unfair to put Miss Langley through all this effort without any warning at all. However, since Ned was being so very cooperative where Miss Vandenhoff was concerned—and since Dovington was desperate for their first meeting to be a pleasant one—he went along with it.

It was, after all, the perfect day for a picnic. The gentle breezed tossed Miss Langley's skirts playfully and the warm sun made her soft skin practically glow. The butter-cream color of her gown accented the golden tones in her hair, and her green eyes sparkled. They turned to fire, though, when she caught him looking at her.

"I hope these preparations are up to your standards, sir," she said curtly when she was forced to stand near him and help with the loading of the hampers. "As you know, we did not have much time to arrange things."

"I'm sure everything will be more than adequate, Miss Langley. My cousin and I appreciate very much that you have indulged us in this."

"I didn't realize I had the option to refuse," she said, shoving an unruly curl back up into her bonnet.

"You always have that option, of course. But I am happy you chose to go along with us on this. In fact... I wonder if I can request a favor."

"Another?"

"Regarding Miss Vandenhoff."

They were very much alone together now, standing behind one of the carriages while the servants moved on to the other.

"And what special accommodation has she requested?" Miss

Langley asked with a telling sigh.

"Er, nothing. Not yet, at least," the earl replied. "I was hoping, though... that is..."

"Yes?"

"Well, as you may have noticed, the young lady does not seem entirely comfortable here. I was hoping you might take her under your wing, as it were, and help her to be... help her to enjoy herself a bit more."

The way she cocked her eyebrow at him and gave a delightful scowl assured him she understood exactly what he meant. And that she had ample doubts about her ability to accomplish such a thing.

"You've been such a remarkable hostess for her already," he went on quickly. "And I know it cannot be easy to have a family of strangers invade your home this way. But my cousin has not yet met Miss Vandenhoff and... well, I was very much hoping he might not find her off-putting today."

She rolled her green eyes and nodded. "Of course. And you think I can just magically make her behave. Certainly sir. I'll just wave my enchanted wand and she'll fall directly in line."

"You hardly need a wand, Miss Langley. You've shown such a kind, understanding nature that surely Miss Vandenhoff will—"

"Save your flattery, sir. I will endeavor to shine the best light possible on Miss Vandenhoff, but not because you ask me. It is simply the proper thing to do."

He liked the way she did not back down even as he stepped closer to her. They were very near one another now, the servants all bustling elsewhere and leaving them markedly alone. He could hardly help himself from taking advantage of the situation. Entertainment had been in short supply for him of late and watching Miss Langley's flashing eyes and dodging her rapier wit had become quite a pleasurable distraction.

"And you always do the proper thing, don't you, Miss Langley?"

"Of course I do. Never doubt it."

"Doubt it? Oh, I'll never do that, Miss Langley. I'm sure when you do finally decide to abandon propriety, there'll be no doubt about it whatsoever."

She narrowed her eyes and grumbled at him. "I gladly invite you to hold your breath for that day, sir."

"Be careful what you invite, Miss Langley."

Her reply—and it would have been stinging, he was certain—was cut off by the giggling arrival of her sister. Miss Renford appeared in the doorway of the house, being escorted out by none other than Ned. And he seemed quite pleased with his role.

"I believe I've located one of our picnickers," he announced.

"He found me in the hallway fretting over my abominable bonnet," Miss Renford tittered. "There was no one around, so we were forced to introduce ourselves."

"And a good thing we did," Ned went on. "I was able to rescue Miss Renford from that dreadful chapeau. The abominable thing was vanquished and this adorable bit was procured to take its place."

Oh good God, but Ned was making cow's eyes at the girl. This was not at all what was planned for the day. Dovington toyed with the idea of demanding Miss Langley find some excuse to keep her bubbling and blushing little sister home, but it was too late. Ned had already met the girl and it would be impossible for him to wipe her from his mind in time to avoid the obvious comparisons to Miss Vandenhoff.

As vibrant and innocent and charming as Miss Renford was, Miss Vandenhoff would merely seem that much more dour and unlikeable. Damn it all. He should have taken steps to avoid this sort of thing.

Too late now, though. Miss Vandenhoff appeared behind them, wearing a frilly gown covered over by a drab, gray colored wrap. Her face was as sour as Miss Renford's was sweet. Her ladies maid cowered behind her carrying a parcel nearly as large as the hampers Miss Langley's servants had packed.

Desperate to salvage what he could of the moment, Dovington stepped up and greeted the young lady before she had time to complain about the sunshine, the scented breezes, or demand the nearby daffodils to be plowed under for being too yellow.

"Ah, here you are, Miss Vandenhoff. How good you look this morning."

"I know. Where should my maid stow my things? I wasn't sure what manner of foods would be offered to us on this outing, so I brought my own. I hope no one minds."

As promised, Miss Langley responded properly and perfectly.

"Of course not. I'm happy our kitchen staff was able to find what you wanted."

Dovington could barely detect that she bit her tongue to keep from indicating what an insult the American had given. As if Miss Langley should provide a less than adequate meal for them! By God, he had half a mind to take Miss Vandenhoff down a notch on her behalf.

He didn't, though. He bit his own tongue and presented his cousin.

"Miss Vandenhoff, may I present my cousin, Edmund Chadburne? He just arrived this morning and it was his idea, as a matter of fact, that we take advantage of the fine weather today for this outing. Ned, Miss Vandenhoff has come all the way from America. She and her family are on holiday here."

Ned had the good sense not to recoil at the uninterested nod he received from Miss Vandenhoff. He bowed just as politely as ever and made a respectable effort to be charming.

"I hope your travel has been well, Miss Vandenhoff. I've often fancied the notion of visiting across the Atlantic myself. Have you any place you would recommend?"

"I've found sea voyage quite nauseating," she replied, walking past him to stand stiffly beside the carriage. "I recommend you stay home if at all possible."

Clearly she had nothing more to say on the matter and Dovington was thankful for that. She waited with her chin in the air for someone to assist her into the carriage. The warm spring air took on a decided chill and the bright sun seemed to dim a few shades.

Dovington caught Miss Langley's eye. This time she didn't flash fire at him or look away in disgust. Instead her expression asked him just how he expected her to make a silk purse out of this pig's ear.

Quite honestly, he had no idea. They were in for it now and there was nothing to be done but survive it. Hoisting his shoulders back and putting on the bravest face possible, he moved to Miss Vandenhoff's side and offered to assist her into the carriage.

"Shall we be off on this adventure, then?" he asked.

One more glance at Miss Langley and he thought he caught her actually smiling. The chit was positively amused by his discomfort. Well, he'd just see how much more amusement he could provide her as the day went on.

Chapter 10

The birds were singing overhead and the carriages rattled along the familiar old road. Their party of five picnickers was crowded into the old square landau while two footmen and Miss Vandenhoff's maid rode along behind them in a separate conveyance carrying the hampers and other supplies for the day's outing. Mariah sat wedged between Ella and Miss Vandenhoff on the seat facing forward, and the two gentlemen sat in the seat facing them.

The hoods were down so they could enjoy the weather, but after a few minutes of uncomfortable silence Mariah was wishing they could put them up again and tell the coachman to race the horses out to their selected picnic area. The sooner this dismal event could be over, the better. Miss Vandenhoff was like a dark cloud hovering over all of them.

"The flowers this year are so lovely," Ella chirped as they rolled past Mrs. Saunders house with her many window boxes and well tended garden.

"Indeed," Mr. Chadburne replied brightly. "I always forget how vivid the colors are here in the country. What is the name of this little village we are coming into?"

"This is Hinders Sundry," Mariah replied. "As you see, not a large village but it has its own market one day each month and the shops provide most of what we need."

"See there?" Ella pointed out as they clattered along the old road. "That shop has the most delightful hair ribbons! Perhaps tomorrow you might like to walk into the village with me, Miss Vandenhoff, and look at them?"

The heiress peered at the shop and then shrugged. "St. Peter warns us about the outward adorning of plaiting the hair and wearing of gold," the heiress replied, though Mariah wasn't entirely sure what she meant by it.

Ella seemed equally confused. She wrinkled up her nose and frowned. "Well, I know they have ribbon, but I don't believe they sell anything gold..."

How on earth was Mariah going to redirect this? She glanced at Ella for support but her sister merely blinked huge blue eyes in mute befuddlement. It seemed for the moment they were all doomed to uncomfortable silence again. Fortunately, Mr. Chadburne came to the rescue.

"How true that often the simplest adornment is the best," he said lightly. "That little grove of trees, for instance, could be in a painting by one of those new romantic artists."

"Oh, but I adore art," Ella said, nearly stumbling over her words on a subject that Mariah knew was very dear to her. "I brought my chalks along today and hope to make some sketches of the views on our outing."

Mr. Chadburne seemed every bit as eager to embrace this subject as Ella had been. "Brilliant idea, Miss Renford. I'm already impatient to see what you'll create for us. Do you always use chalk or do you dabble in watercolors, as well?"

"You are a lover of art, Mr. Chadburne?" Mariah asked, happy to capitalize on such a cheery topic at last.

"My mother is, actually," he replied. "She's forever forcing me to take her to galleries and such. I'm hardly an expert on the matter, but I will admit to having an appreciation for the talent and craft required for painting or sketching."

Ella agreed whole heartedly and at last it seemed as if the group might embark on actual conversation. It was not to be, however. The earl made the foolhardy mistake of asking Miss Vandenhoff for her thoughts on the subject.

"I think the time spent smearing paint could much better be put to other uses and the vast sums of money wasted to support such activities could surely go toward more productive efforts," the American replied in her usually snippy tones.

Mariah glared at the earl. How could he possibly expect her to help make the chit appear to advantage if he went about tossing questions at her? Clearly her contrary nature had to be treated much more carefully. She needed to be managed with extreme caution and certainly not given opportunity to rant over questions thrown at her willy-nilly.

Somehow Mariah simply had to find a subject that the girl could agree with. There must be something! Miss Vandenhoff could not possibly be negative about *everything* on the planet, could she?

"Well, I certainly admit that any time I might spend smearing paint could certainly be put to better use," Mariah said. "I fear I have no talent for it whatsoever, though I am glad that some people seem to find enjoyment from it. Mrs. Wakefield, for instance," she said, pointing at the large home they were just now passing by, "has quite a good eye for such things. Just a few months ago she had a portrait commissioned for her grandchildren. I should think that such a gift as that would be quite a good use of artistic talent."

Miss Vandenhoff appeared not to agree. "And Mrs. Wakefield lives in this house? It hardly seems grand enough for a family who can afford such luxuries."

"This is the rectory," Mariah explained. "Mr. Wakefield is our vicar, although he is getting on in years and now shares his duties with our new curate."

"And still he can pay for such things as portraits? What a vicar he must be. Does this new curate live in such imposing style as well?"

Clearly there was no pleasing the girl. "No, I'm happy to say the new curate lives alone in a very small house with no portraits at all. Is that as it should be?"

Miss Vandenhoff shrugged. "Pity your parish cannot care for him better."

Exasperating hussy! Mariah had to clench her fists as well as her teeth to keep from grabbing her guest and throttling her. How could the girl possibly think she was any sort of decent company? It was inconceivable that anyone—even an American—could be so boldly rude and unlikable.

As for Lord Dovington—well, he was equally exasperating. By heavens, when she glared at him in irate frustration, the man actually smiled at her. He seemed perfectly at ease, amused by her aggravation, even. What nerve, when he was the very one she suffered such appalling treatment for! She folded her arms over her chest and sank back into her seat.

Fine. If he could find such a distasteful exchange compelling, then she would happily let him. But she would not participate. If he was determined to marry himself to someone spouting off bitter retorts all day long, he was perfectly welcome to do so. He'd simply have to do it without any assistance from her.

"You seem to be of strong conviction, Miss Vandenhoff," he said, unphased by the reproach on the girl's face. "I am glad you feel emboldened to express your true feelings on things. Too often ladies are trained to keep silent on serious matters, but not you. How refreshing that you are exceptional in that way, wouldn't you say, Ned?"

"Oh, er, yes," his cousin replied quickly, after receiving a subtle elbow to his ribs. "Exceptional, to say the least."

For a moment it seemed Miss Vandenhoff wasn't sure how to take this odd sort of compliment. Mariah quite enjoyed seeing her at a loss, but soon her usual sourness returned and she curled her lip at the men.

"You are free to form your opinions of me, of course. I, however, do not trust in pleasing men, but God, which trieth our hearts."

Mariah hoped, for the girl's sake, God didn't spend too much time trying hers. He'd very likely find himself offended. Fortunately, though, the earl took Miss Vandenhoff's censure in stride.

"You seem to be fond of quoting scripture," he noted. "I take it you are rather devout?"

"I am, sir. I find the study of scripture to be a most rewarding application."

Mariah bit her tongue before stating the obvious. Whatever scripture Miss Vandenhoff must be studying, it certainly hadn't had much of an impact. Nothing Mariah could recall from Mr. Wakefield's readings mentioned sacred mandates for rudeness and affront. Perhaps the translation was different in America, though.

"It is an admirable undertaking, no doubt," his lordship said.

"Study to shew thyself approved unto God, a workman that needeth not to be ashamed," Miss Vandenhoff replied.

Mariah cringed, but the earl surprised her by avoiding the temptation to ridicule or to shew himself completely *un*approved. Apparently the man knew a bit of scripture himself.

"Don't forget, Miss Vandenhoff, we are also told that of making many books there is no end; and much study is a weariness of the flesh."

Miss Vandenhoff was duly impressed. "I see you are a bit of a scholar yourself, sir."

"I paid attention in school when it suited me," he said. "My cousin, however, is much more learned in such matters than I am. For a time he considered pursuing ordination, didn't you, Ned?"

At last they had hit on a subject that enthralled Miss Vandenhoff. Her eyes grew wide and she gazed at Mr. Chadburne.

"You, sir? Are you no longer considering the church, then?"

She seemed disappointed in that, but listened intently as Mr. Chadburne explained that other duties had arisen to interfere with his religious pursuits. When he mentioned that it would have been a good number of years before he could have counted on a living, he received a warning glance from the earl. Mariah did not let that go unnoticed.

Apparently the topic of Mr. Chadburne's clerical expectations was not to be discussed. Very likely that meant either this earl or his father had been forced to sell off any living possessed by the Dovington estate. If Mr. Chadburne had indeed completed his ordination, there would have been no where for him to go. Pity.

Where most grand families held vicarages to offer the younger sons, apparently this was just one more area where Dovington was lacking. Poor Mr. Chadburne could not look forward to support from his own family. Once again, the fact of Dovington's diminished condition threatened to give Miss Vandenhoff just one more reason to disregard him. Mariah would have to re-involve herself in this conversation to help

73

rescue the man, drat it all.

But that notion was more easily dreamed than done. Miss Vandenhoff and Mr. Chadburne were so embroiled in their discussion of philosophical differences in points of doctrine that Mariah could not get a word in edgewise. Oh, but this was terrible! The heiress was pleasantly animated for the first time since her arrival, and her attentions were clearly pinned on Mr. Chadburne, not his desperately eligible cousin.

Finally the conversation hit a lull and Mariah was just about to pipe up with something—anything—to distract them, but his lordship apparently had the same idea. Instead of successfully regaining Miss Vandenhoff's attention for himself, though, he posed a question for Mariah.

"It seems this side of your village is not nearly so well kept as the other," he said, indicating the overgrown hedgerows and tumbled state of the walls lining the roadway as they left the village behind and were, once again, traveling through farm lands.

"These lands are someone else's, sir. On the other side of the village, the area we have already been through, those farmers are tenants of... well, they are yours, actually."

This truly seemed to surprise him. "Mine? You mean to say when your step-father bought The Grove he thought he was purchasing the farm lands as well?"

"He did, and he managed them very well all those years, if I do say."

"Indeed, they appear to be thriving, but... your step-father has been gone three full years now, has he not? Many of the improvements I noticed in those areas appear very recent? Who has been managing the tenants in his absence?"

"I have, of course. I told you that."

"I thought you meant you'd been managing the household," he explained. "I assumed you'd been overseeing the purchase of candles and mutton for the larder, that sort of thing."

"I have. And the well-being of tenants, and the upkeep of walls, and the condition of our lesser roadways, and new channels being dug for additional irrigation... I assumed you understood what was needed in the oversight of an estate."

"I do, of course. I just never knew... that is, my father's papers were in such disarray I did not realize this estate was as large as it apparently is. You are certain all these things you've told me are accurate?"

"You think I know less about my home than you do, sir? When I've lived here for twenty years and been primary overseer of it all for three?"

"No, I meant... I will clearly have to look into things."

"You do that. When you are content that everything is as I just told you, then you might perhaps let me know."

Drat. Had she really just informed him that Renford Hall was even more valuable than he'd known? She'd let her pride carry her away. He'd started her on the subject and she'd rambled on about her glorious achievements. Now he would not only be trying to evict her family, but very likely all their tenants, as well, in his eagerness to pillage his newfound property for momentary profit. Oh, but how foolish could she be?

So far this picnic was turning into quite the disaster, she was sorry to say. Miss Vandenhoff was being most unpleasant, the earl was practically rubbing his hands together and salivating with greed over his new information, and now Mr. Chadburne was quite contentedly drawing all of Miss Vandenhoff's attention for himself. If any part of this day could be worse, she didn't know what it might be.

Chapter 11

This picnic was going even better than planned. Dovington couldn't imagine what might be better: Miss Vandenhoff was enthralled by Ned's discourse, the weather was pleasant, the little Miss Renford was genial and, for the most part, silent, and now Miss Langley had just informed him he was wealthier than he thought. He'd had no idea the lands attached to The Grove were such promising properties. It remained to be seen exactly what profit could be got from any of these, but he had to admit on first glance Miss Langley appeared to have been a most excellent steward for these past years.

No wonder she was loathe to leave the place. Clearly her labors had not been done out of duty alone, but out of an honest appreciation and concern. He could almost feel remorse for having to put the girl out of her home.

Almost. Too many years of his own disappointments made it easy to ignore that of others. He would simply not allow himself to think on those lines. Miss Langley was young and attractive, and she'd shown herself more than capable. Clearly she could do well anywhere she landed. To assuage whatever guilt he might feel, he'd simply make sure she landed well.

And far enough away from him that he could forget ever having laid eyes on her.

Perhaps he ought to make certain Ned forgot about her, as well. It seemed Ned's conversation with Miss Vandenhoff had run its course and now Ned was easily swayed when Miss Langley distracted him with questions about whichever useless things seemed to pop into her head. For some reason, she suddenly wanted to know if Ned was a frequent visitor to the British Museum. Had he seen the Elgin Marbles? Was he familiar with the opera? Did he find the amusements at Vauxhall as delightful as the newspapers proclaimed? Was he there for the hot air balloon assent she'd read something about?

Ned seemed only too happy to give detailed responses to her questions and Dovington tried to catch the girl's eye to warn her off of him, but she was having none of it. In fact, her only response seemed to have been to pull him into their discussion, as well.

"Surely you have spent much time in London, sir," she asked as if she were truly interested. "What do you find the most interesting feature of the city?"

"Interesting? Well, I'd have to say—"

"St. Paul's, correct? Oh, but I've heard it's magnificent. To imagine a dome of such monumental proportions is truly amazing."

"Er, yes, I believe it is quite—"

Again she cut off his reply, which was not going to be about St. Paul's. Instead of merely interrupting him, though, now she included Miss Vanderhoff. In fact, it was as if she intentionally included the dubious miss and then passed her off deftly to Dovington.

"Surely even in America, Miss Vandenhoff, you've hear of our great cathedral?" she said pointedly. "Come, my lord, do tell her all about the wonders of St. Paul's."

With Miss Vandenhoff's skeptical eye on him now, there was little he could do but answer in the most genial way possible. "It is very large, for a church."

"So I've heard," Miss Vandenhoff commented. "Perhaps it would be better to use such a space to house the homeless and indigent, which I've heard London is quite full of."

Damn, this conversation was *not* going in the right direction. He looked to Miss Langley for help—she was the one who'd made a muck of things, after all—but she'd already turned her attentions back onto Ned and was busily engaging him in discussion with her sister, asking what places he might recommend their family visit at some point. There was nothing Dovington could do but try to unruffle Miss Vanderhoff's feathers.

"Is that what is done in America?" he asked in all sincerity. "Religious facilities are turned over to be used as workhouses for the poor?"

Apparently this was the wrong thing to ask. He wasn't even certain what she found so offensive in his question, but she spouted off more scripture, platitudes, and even lines from something she called a Constitution. The point, as best he could gather, was that she whole-heartedly disagreed with him and everything about him. What could be done to alter this opinion, he was afraid to ask.

Ned and Miss Langley were no help at all. They carried on very peacefully in their discussion of London's joys and amusements. Dovington wished them all to Hades and was about to say so out loud when Miss Langley finally took her attentions from Ned and called to their driver.

"Here we are! You can leave us out here, Jos." Now she smiled at the group in the carriage and waved her arms wide to indicated the sprawling countryside around them. "I thought this spot would suit our purposes perfectly. Isn't the view here irresistibly romantic?"

Their carriage pulled up to a halt and Dovington glanced around. Indeed, her estimation appeared accurate. This was an excellent spot for a picnic.

The grounds rolled away gently, sloping down to a picturesque stream bubbling and sparkling in the bright sun. Birds thrilled in the boughs above them, the grass grew lush and green, and wildflowers dotted the scene, casting fragrance into the Spring-warmed breeze. It was the perfect spot, indeed, for picnickers, artists, or lovers. As all of them were here to picnic, and since Miss Renford had brought along her chalk to play artist for them today, that meant the only players their group lacked were the lovers. But not for long, he vowed to himself.

Ned and Miss Vandenhoff would play their roles here well; he'd make sure of it. In order for that to happen, though, Miss Langley would need to be distracted in some manner. He wasn't overly concerned about facilitating that, however. She was a female, wasn't she? Indeed she was; very much so. And this location truly was just as she'd said: *irresistibly romantic*.

The earl was being especially considerate as they set up and then settled in to enjoy the picnic. Mariah didn't want to be impressed, but she was. The man was being gracious and helpful and everything gentlemanly. He spoke respectfully to the servants and was carefully tending the ladies' needs, positioning blankets and cushions and taking care that no food or drink was spilled that might spoil anyone's clothing. It appeared that even Miss Vandenhoff could find no fault and she fell into silence as conversation centered on Ella and her chalks once again.

It seemed Mr. Chadburne did, indeed, have a great interest in art and he peppered Ella with questions about her efforts. Ella, of course, was all too happy to respond. Mariah supposed she ought to interrupt them and somehow turn focus back onto Miss Vandenhoff in such a way that the earl might engage her in conversation, but her past attempts at that had been met with such failure that she was happy, for now, to allow Mr. Chadburne and Ella to carry the discourse. Sometimes concession must be made for the sake of peace. Hopefully this time of pleasantry would allow for a bit of a cooling off that might put Miss Vandenhoff more in mind to look on the earl with more tolerant eyes.

He certainly was doing his part to make himself more tolerable, she had to admit. His expression was friendly and his occasional contributions to the conversation were amiable and engaging. Oh, and the way the breezed played with his dark hair while the sunlight positively glinted in his eyes... it might be easy to forget what an ogre he truly was. If Miss Vandenhoff did not find herself softening just a bit toward the man after this, then clearly there was no hope for the girl.

Or any of them, unfortunately. Mariah would have to stop enjoying the peace and get back to the business of matching these two if she wanted Ella to be able to continue sketching this countryside or Mamma to remain in the home she had loved for twenty years now. As nice as it was to sit idly and soak in the lovely day, there was work to be done and no better time than the present to do it.

"Do you find the countryside here to be much different from rural places where you are from, Miss Vandenhoff?" she asked, convinced there could be nothing inflammatory in her words.

"The farming areas are not dramatically different," the American replied in blessedly calm, civilized tones. "Though I admit to spending most of my time in the city. When my family does leave for holiday, we usually stay at our summer home on the shore and that is, of course, very different from here."

"We are fairly near the shore here, aren't we?" Mr. Chadburne asked. "Two years ago I went to stay with friends near Portsmouth. That must be within an easy journey of here, I should think."

Ella replied before Mariah could. "Indeed, it is a very easy journey to the shore. My father used to take us there often on days when the weather was warm. Mariah and I would venture out in the bathing machines while Papa and Mamma would relax on the beach."

"As I recall, though, you always refused to come down the steps actually into the water," Mariah reminded.

But Ella had a ready reply for that. "And all you ever seemed to care about was smuggling carrots for the horses that pulled us into the waters. I think you enjoyed playing with them more than you did the ocean that we had gone all that way to see."

Even Miss Vandenhoff seemed to find the story amusing and the tone within the group was decidedly light. Still, though, the earl appeared to be hesitant to speak to Miss Vandenhoff himself. Instead he was more inclined to have his cousin make pleasantries for him, constantly remarking to the younger man that he should tell the ladies of this tale or that. Mr. Chadburne obliged, entertaining them with stories of his various misadventures while angling in chalk streams, or losing at a bet and having to spend an entire night in an abandoned abbey that everyone swore was quite haunted.

Miss Vandenhoff scoffed at the mention of ghosts, but Ella was quite enthralled with the idea. Mr. Chadburne seemed to be enjoying the attentions of both young ladies and was clearly embellishing as he described mournful moans and clanking chain and misty specters floating in the darkness. The man was a gifted storyteller and was making himself out to be far more amiable and interesting than his lordship. Certainly he was making Mariah's task harder for her. She'd best do something soon to distract Miss Vandenhoff from the younger man's virtues.

Their meal was done and Ella's box of chalks and her drawing papers lay nearby. That seemed an excellent tool for distraction. Mariah latched onto it when there was a brief lull in the conversation.

"Have you decided what view you would like to sketch today, Ella?" she asked. "I can help you set up wherever you might like to be."

"Oh, well I suppose I can just begin sketching from here," Ella replied.

Drat. How was staying here with the whole group going to do anything to put Miss Vandenhoff into a romantic mood toward Lord Dovington? Somehow she'd have to get the man involved in helping himself in this cause. Honestly, but it seemed he didn't have the first clue about wooing a female.

"I suppose it is a good scene," Mariah admitted. "But there are other very lovely views, as well. Perhaps his lordship and Miss Vandenhoff would be interested in walking along that slight ridge there. Just beyond those trees, as I recall, is a perfect vantage for viewing the church spire and the lands stretching toward Renford Hall."

"I'm not very much given to walking just now," Miss Vandenhoff said. "I prefer to sit here, thank you."

"Well, I'd very much like to see this view you mention, Miss Langley," the earl said. "Perhaps the others can entertain themselves here and you might show me the way?"

Botheration, but this man must have cotton for brains! Did he not realize this was no way to win his fair maiden? Leaving her to sit with his charming young cousin was distinctly the *wrong* thing to do if he had any hopes of attaching her for himself. What could he be thinking?

Perhaps she ought to explain things to him. In private.

"Very well, my lord. If the others are content to stay here and keep my sister company, I will show you the view. I suppose you are quite interested in seeing the boundaries of your lands, and this will provide excellent position for that."

"Lead the way, then, Miss Langley."

Trying not to huff in frustration as she did so, she led him away from their picnic area and toward the high ground that ran as a rise along the top of the slope over the stream. The ridge took a gentle turn where a copse of trees grew from a rocky gap and it wasn't long before they were out of sight from their group. Mariah would have preferred to keep the others safely in view, but in order to show the earl what his greedy eyes wished to see, this was the direction she was forced to go.

At least it would provide opportunity for her to chastise him on his lack of social skills. It was inconceivable that a man who seemed so sure of himself and who, well, who looked the way he did, should be so very inept in that area. Perhaps, though, it was due to his outward appearance that he had never needed to learn the finer arts of wooing a lady. Perhaps he was simply used to ladies throwing themselves at him. Well, clearly he would have to expand his repertoire if he expected to get anywhere with the American heiress.

"I see the church spire from here," he noted, pointing toward the nestle of rooftops peeping through trees down in the valley below. "And beyond that, over there, are those the chimneys of The Grove?"

"Renford Hall, yes. Our lands... that is, *your* lands, go as far as that distant tree line there, and all the way to the river on the far side. You cannot see that from here, but this farm house you see with the thatched roof is the nearest edge of the property."

"Indeed, that is quite an expanse. I had no idea."

"No, it seems you have no idea about a lot of things," she said. "Miss Vandenhoff, for example... I'm not certain things are going quite the way we hoped."

"You don't? But she hasn't insulted any of us for more than an hour now. I think that marks great progress, don't you?"

A smile played at the corners of his lips and his eyes sparkled when they fixed on her. Heavens, but if the man could ever be bothered to look at Miss Vandenhoff in this manner, surely she would fall under his spell in that moment. As it was,

Mariah had to glance away quickly for her own personal well-being.

"I don't know if it is progress in the right direction, though. Aren't you concerned that your cousin is a bit too..."

"A bit too *what*, Miss Langley?"

"Well, he talks a lot. Have you not noticed?"

"You do not find that ingratiating?"

"I have nothing against him and he seems perfectly charming. It's just that to compare the two of you... well, you must admit you are not very much alike."

"Are we supposed to be?"

"No, of course not. It's just that when ladies are involved it is safe to assume that not every gentleman will appeal to every lady."

"So you have been considering our appeal and comparing us. How interesting. Tell me, then, where do I rank, in your estimation?"

"You? Well, that's what I wanted to discuss with you."

"I am eager to hear your opinion on the matter. Would you have me be more of a conversationalist like my cousin, or should I do better as a man of action?"

He was standing very close to her now and it was oddly difficult to breathe. She tried to raise her eyes up to meet his, but somehow her gaze remained stuck on the broad expanse of his chest and the powerful spread of his shoulders. He'd abandoned the full black attire she'd been used to seeing him in and today he wore crisp white linen, his cravat tied in a careless knot just below his chin. His chin... yes, she could get her eyes up to his chin and appreciate the firm set of his jaw, the amused quirk to his lips. Indeed, the man hardly needed to rely on conversation to highlight his appeal.

Action. Of course. That's what was needed where Miss Vandenhoff was concerned. Time was of the essence and clearly conversation was not the man's forte. He should simply sweep the heiress off her feet and have done with it. He must know how to do that, mustn't he?

"Conversation can only go so far, don't you think? Surely by now it is time for action, my lord."

Could it be possible that he was even closer to her now? She could feel the sun's heat radiating off of him. His eyes still sparked, but this time it was the smolder of dancing embers she saw in them. And they drew her. Where she hadn't been able to meet them before, now that she did she was held there, her gaze captured by his and perfectly content to remain there.

Too late, she realized his eyes weren't the only thing holding her. Somehow his hands had come up to touch her, to rest on her shoulders and bring her slowly toward him. She blinked, but that did nothing to break the spell she was under. The rest of the world suddenly seemed very, very far away and she was only aware of him.

"How about this action?" he asked softly, trailing his fingers over her shoulder, along her collar bone, and up to her cheek where he brushed her skin gently.

Her voice was hopelessly gone so she merely nodded. By heavens, if he were to do this to Miss Vandenhoff it would most certainly work in his favor!

"And perhaps even this?" he said, pressing her close against him as he stroked her lightly at the nape of her neck.

Oh, but she liked that. Of course she shouldn't like it, yet there was no denying that she did. The man might be an utter failure at conversation, but he certainly did know a thing or two about action. Her dratted eyelids seemed to forget that now was probably not the best time for her to be taking lessons from him. They drooped involuntarily, falling entirely shut as he pulled her tighter against his broad, heated body.

"And this?" he murmured.

First she felt his warm breath against her face, and then his lips touched hers. Sparks like tiny tingles of lightning flashed inside of her. They shot through her limbs, igniting her nerves and prickling outward through her skin. Her knees sagged and she wrapped her arms around the earl to keep herself from crumbling. Also, to keep him from ending this before she could fully comprehend what it was.

His lips brushed hers. She waited there, motionless, willing her eyes to open but happy they did not so she could concentrate fully on the man's lips. They gave merely a tentative nibble at first, but as her heart pounded in anticipation that quickly turned into something more. She was at a loss how to respond, but he held her so closely and controlled her so effortlessly that soon she knew exactly what to do.

She kissed him back.

Her lips gave in to his, yielding for him and yet at the same time eager to devour him for herself. The lightning continued to race inside her, setting fires inside her that burned in the most delightful way. It hardly mattered that she couldn't even breathe just now.

It must have mattered to Dovington, though. Eventually he pulled back from her, breaking off the kiss and allowing her some much-needed oxygen to clear her brain. She still clung to him as the world spun around her.

"I quite agree with you, Miss Langley," he said when her eyes drifted open just enough to gaze up at him. "Conversation is highly overrated. I shall rely on action whenever possible now."

It took a moment to collect her thoughts and put words into some sense of order. And her voice? It took another moment longer to find that.

"If you rely on actions like those, sir, you will have Miss Vandenhoff swooning at your feet in no time. Just as you hoped, she'll be begging to attach her fortune to your title."

His classical brow furrowed and for a moment he appeared confused. "Her fortune with *my* title? But I—"

The nearby bark of a dog startled them both. His arms tightened around her but she could turn her head enough to see a black and white collie dog trotting up the sloping hillside toward them. She recognized the animal immediately and knew the dog's owner could not be far behind.

Realization of where she was and what she was doing slammed into her and she pushed herself away from the earl. He let her go but the confusion on his face only deepened. It took but a moment to be replaced by understanding once a man's form could be seen coming into view on the path alongside the stream below them. The earl swore under his breath and stepped away from her.

The dog raced ahead of her master and came to dance around

the two on the ridge. The man below waved and called out a greeting. Mariah steadied herself and waved at him. He began heading their way.

The collie nuzzled Dovington's leg as he patted its head. His smoldering glance toward Mariah made her suddenly dizzy. She'd best douse any lingering heat immediately, before their guest might reach them and notice.

"This is Bess," she said, indicating the dog. "And that is her master, Mr. Ben Skrewd. He is our curate."

Chapter 12

So he'd very nearly been discovered by the local curate, manhandling Miss Langley and enjoying every moment of it? Well, thank heavens for barking dogs, Dovington supposed. Truth be told, though, he would have much rather been *un*interrupted altogether. When Miss Langley said she preferred action to conversation, she hadn't been lying. Her eager response had been all the conversation he needed to know this was not going to be the last time he got the woman into his arms.

For now, though, he'd best get his mind off that and behave in a civilized manner. The young curate had been introduced as Mr. Skrewd and he seemed amiable enough. Perhaps even too much, as it seemed he and Miss Langley were on very friendly terms.

They joined the rest of the group and for a time all attention was on the simple, but very nicely done, chalk sketch that Miss Renford had been creating. Ned was, perhaps, being overly effusive in his praise of the girl's talent, but Dovington would not fault him for that. Anything that might give reason to Miss Vanderhoff for approving of Ned's behavior was commendable.

The pleasantries and chatter went on far longer than the earl could manage, though. His focus was continually wandering off to consider the soft curves of Miss Langley's form, the elegant arc of her neck and the recollection of just how enticing those elements had been in his arms, under his touch. Her full lips were still pink with the glow from his kiss and he could barely take his eyes from them.

When he finally was distracted from her it was to realize she'd been asking him a question.

"Will you, my lord?" she repeated.

His first instinct was to consent to whatever she might be asking him, but good sense won out and he thought he might do well to at least clarify first.

"I... er, will I what?"

"Attend our ball," she replied, her eyes flashing and her voice clipped.

A ball? Good God, was that what the group had been rambling about? He must have been much deeper in thought than he'd known. The last thing he wanted to attend was some country ball with a pack of curious rustics showing up to ogle him. Then again, it would be an excellent way to put Ned and Miss Vandenhoff together. He hated to admit it, but Miss Langley did seem to have a good idea here.

"Yes, I should think that if you are planning a ball, I will likely attend," he conceded. "When are you to schedule this thing?"

"In three days!" Miss Renford chimed eagerly. "I don't think that is too short a time at all. It does not have to be a fancy ball, and it would be so wonderful to finally have a group of young people all together for such an occasion."

Apparently Miss Langley had doubted the notion of pulling together such an undertaking in but three days, and the earl was tempted to agree. Who would even attempt such a thing? But Miss Langley sighed and gave in to her sister.

"I suppose you are correct," she said with a smile. "We rarely have such friends in our company and I agree that a ball would be just the thing. Somehow we'll make it work."

Miss Renford clapped her hands in excitement, chalk dust flying up in a puff around her. Even Miss Vandenhoff agreed that perhaps a ball would not be the worst thing they could do with their time. Ned clearly approved, and the curate offered to invite some musicians he knew. There would be a ball in three days' time at Renford Hall and, oddly enough, Lord Dovington was actually looking forward to it.

Not only would he have an excuse to dance with Miss Langley, but there could be no better time than a ball to announce an engagement. All his efforts here would pay off and the Vandenhoff fortune would soon be at the disposal of the future Earl of Dovington. The family name would be saved and he could lay down his heavy burden, finally.

He would, of course, have to set Miss Langley straight on one tiny detail. It seemed she was under the mistaken impression that he was hoping to win Miss Vandenhoff for himself. No wonder the chit had been so determined to interrupt every time Ned seemed to be making some headway. He had to hide a chuckle as he thought of the ridiculous misunderstanding.

As if *he* could ever marry Miss Vandenhoff! What a thought. Once they were back at the house, he'd have to find opportunity to get Miss Langley alone and inform her of the situation.

If he could pry her away from this curate, of course. Dash it all, but the chit seemed absolutely joined at the hip with this man now that he'd turned up. Yes, the dog was a pleasant addition to their little group, but Dovington found he could not enjoy Mr. Skrewd's presence.

Certainly not nearly as much as Miss Langley appeared to.

After surviving the afternoon's outing and arriving home without making the mistake of finding herself alone with the earl again, Mariah escaped up to her room for a couple hours of much needed rest. Not that she'd actually been able to rest. No, her mind had been far too busy, a jumble of planning and concern and, well, memories of certain things she was now desperate to forget.

The earl had kissed her! Indeed, he'd kissed her quite soundly and she'd done nothing to stop him. In fact, she was quite certain she'd made his work easier for him, pressing herself up against him and holding on, letting her lips explore his as if she were eager for whatever more he might offer. Good heavens, but if Mr. Skrewd and Bess had not come along she could only imagine what she might have let herself get up to.

The man was a sorcerer. All her life she'd taken great care never to let herself be swayed by such things. She'd never even dreamed that she might actually enjoy it! Now here it was dinner time already and she still could hardly think of anything else.

Something was different inside her, something deep in her

core was humming now and the more she thought of the earl's flashing smile, his penetrating gaze, or the masterful way his lips caressed hers and sent her mind soaring off in a hundred new directions... well, the humming grew louder. How on earth was she going to sit at table with him tonight and not give herself away?

But the dinner hour was on them and there was no avoiding it. She'd dressed in one of her nicer gowns—simply because it was handy and the maid had suggested it, not because she knew it flattered her figure just so—and made sure her hair looked especially tidy. One of Ella's ribbons matched the gown perfectly so it only made sense to have it woven into her curls. Nothing special. Her last furtive glance in the mirror assured her she looked more than presentable.

Coming down the main staircase, she was just in time for the arrival of Mr. Skrewd. He'd been invited to join them tonight and Mariah was exceedingly glad for it. They'd have a large party and that would certainly help keep focus off of her. She smiled as the footman ushered Mr. Skrewd inside and collected his things.

"How nice to have you join us tonight," she greeted, allowing him to take her hand and bow over it politely.

"Thank you so much for inviting me. I hope I am on time," he replied. "I know you have guests and I would hate to make anyone wait on me."

"You are directly on time. Here, come into the drawing room and we'll see who else is gathering now."

She led him in through the nearby doorway and was slightly surprised to find the room empty. Apparently all her agitation had prodded her to be quick in her preparations and she was the first of their household to come down. No matter. This would give her an excellent opportunity to cover an important matter with Mr. Skrewd.

"I see we are the first. Perhaps, then, we can discuss that little item we've been working on. How are things going for it?"

"Oh, you mean Bess's pups?" he said, not comprehending her careful use of hushed tones and subtlety. "They are quite well! The one with the white spot on its nose that you selected for your sister is very much the little clown, actually."

"Shh! It is to be a surprise, remember? I haven't mentioned anything about it to Ella, so please do not give me away. I do so want her to be surprised."

"Ah yes, of course." He dropped his voice and took a step closer to her to preserve their privacy. "I'm so sorry. You are kindness indeed to think of her that way."

"She has long wanted a pet. Mamma was very easy to convince when I told her the sad story of how you rescued poor Bess when she was abandoned. You are quite kind yourself, I daresay. But now you have all these fat little pups who need homes. Have you had any luck with that?"

"I have, thankfully. Your farmer, Mr. Turner, will take one, and Mrs. Smith out on the Southhampton road will take another. Soon they will all be spoken for, I believe."

"I'm so happy to hear it."

"They ought to be ready to go in just a few days."

"Really? Do you think even by the day of our ball? I should love to surprise Ella after the ball."

"Yes, they will be ready by then. She will never suspect a puppy *and* a ball on the same day, will she?"

They huddled together to plot their surprise. Mariah asked what sort of food she ought to have on hand, and Mr. Skrewd told her of the antics she would need to expect. Shoes, apparently, would become prime targets if she did not keep them carefully up, and there would need to be frequent trips out of doors—even at night!—until the pup learned to control itself better.

So deep in discussion were they that she did not even notice someone had come into the room with them. Lord Dovington's loud *ahem* caught her attention and made her jump as if caught in some childish mischief. Heat reared up in her cheeks and she prayed he might not notice.

"Pardon me," he said. "Am I interrupting?"

She smiled politely in his general direction. He looked so elegant in his tidy dinner attire that she didn't dare meet his eyes. He might detect just how pleased she was to see him.

"No, of course not," she replied. "We are just waiting for

dinner to be announced. It seems we are head of the others."

"So I see. How fortunate that you've kept yourselves well entertained in everyone's absence."

She did not like what his tone implied. "It's amazing that polite conversation can be so engaging, isn't it? You ought to try it some time, my lord."

"Polite conversation? No, I much prefer actions, Miss Langley."

The knowing smirk he gave her nearly seared a hole in the wallpaper behind her. She was enormously thankful that her mother and sister appeared in the doorway behind him at that point. He was prevented from tormenting her any more, though her guilty conscience knew she certainly deserved it for that dreadful lapse in judgment just hours ago.

"I see our guest has arrived already," Mamma said, nodding to the earl as she entered the room but then fixing her smile on the curate. "How nice to have you with us again, Mr. Skrewd."

"I always enjoy my time with you, Mrs. Renford. Thank you so much for including me. I look forward to meeting the rest of the party. Miss Vandenhoff and her parents will be joining us, I assume?"

"Of course," Mamma replied. "Ah, here they are now."

Everyone shifted as the Vandenhoffs entered the room and made themselves comfortable. Introductions were made and Mr. Vandenhoff asked how the picnic had gone, giving everyone opportunity to rave about the excellent views and even more excellent weather. Thankfully, nothing was said about the fact that Mariah was lured off alone with a certain glowering gentleman.

She would not look at him and give him the satisfaction of knowing that every word spoken about the picnic today served only to make her relive over and over again those foolish moments in his arms. He would never know how it affected her, and she would certainly never allow it to happen again. No matter how much she might want to.

"But where is Mr. Chadburne?" Ella asked after a few casual minutes.

"I believe he went into the village," the earl replied. "He said something about posting some letters. I expect he'll be back any minute now. I know he would never want to keep any of us waiting."

He turned a generous smile on Miss Vandenhoff and Mariah was most disappointed in herself when she detected the slightest hint of jealously. How aggravating that the heiress should get such a pleasant expression from the man while she herself merited only a lecherous smirk. Not that she wanted anything at all from him, smiling or smirking or otherwise. No indeed.

All she was after where the earl was concerned was to have him out of her house. She'd do well to keep herself firmly reminded of this. Dinner tonight would provide a well needed opportunity to progress toward that goal and with Miss Vandenhoff seeming less anxious and ill-tempered than usual, things were looking up.

If Mariah could only stop looking up at the earl. Every time she caught sight of him across the room her heart toppled over sideways inside her chest. The dreadful man had no right to do this to her. Even though he likely had no idea of it, she vowed hold it against him. Forever.

"I'm so sorry I'm late!"

It was Mr. Chadburne bursting in, hat in hand and a boyish grin on his face. Mamma assured him he was right on time and, sure enough, the housekeeper announced dinner just at that very moment. In the most orderly, genial fashion the earl led them in to dinner and everything seemed—for these few moments, at least—right with the world.

Chapter 13

Miss Langley seemed very pleased with herself, sitting there beside her curate, dressed in a rather revealing sage-colored gown that showed off her milky complexion and made the green of her eyes sparkle like emeralds. Her smiles were sparkling, too, as she tossed her fair curls and laughed at every inane little thing Mr. Skrewd mumbled at her. Dovington could have choked the young man, if he wasn't certain lightning would come out of the sky and smite him for such a thing. Hell, he likely deserved smiting simply for the things he was thinking right now.

He wanted to wipe those dazzling smiles right off Miss Langley's face, to haul her off into some dark, distant recess of this house and make her forget all about her fresh-faced, doting cleric. What sort of vixen was she, anyway, that she could kiss Dovington with such willful abandon in one moment, then instantly turn and throw herself at the reverend in the next? And why, in God's name, if she must throw herself at someone, would she choose Mr. Skrewd?

There was one good thing from it, though. With Mr. Skrewd yapping at her side she found very little time to foolishly try to fling Miss Vandenhoff at Dovington's feet. Oh, she was doing her best to keep the heiress cheerful and drawn into whatever conversation circulated in their area of the table, but due to the seating arrangement that kept her fairly limited to promoting discourse between her sister, Miss Vandenhoff, and the virtuous curate. He, of course, was fairly beaming at the attentions of so many young ladies.

Dovington was left to concentrate on facilitating pleasantries between Ned and the older members of their group. It was the perfect opportunity to see that his cousin was firmly planted in

Mr. Vandenhoff's good graces. He had to credit the young man for playing his part well. Ned gave due reverence to the Vandenhoffs and was especially attentive to their hostess, Mrs. Renford. By the time the final courses were brought out, it was clear she sat firmly in his pocket. Surely Mr. Vandenhoff would admire such behavior and want no one better for his son-in-law.

All that was needed now was to give the young people some time together and victory would be won. Dovington could make whatever arrangements were required, get Ned properly married, then rid himself of Miss Langley and her distracting complexion. And other parts.

Mariah declared dinner a success. In her own mind, of course, but clearly things were going much, much better than they had last night. Mr. Skrewd proved a delightful addition to their group and Miss Vandenhoff was almost to the point of being pleasant. Perhaps her earlier discontent had been all owing to the burden of travel, after all.

The gentlemen had not kept the ladies waiting long before joining them in the drawing room after dinner and the atmosphere was still jovial and inviting. Ella was graciously keeping Miss Vandenhoff entertained as they turned pages in the large book of dogs that had been left out. Mr. Skrewd and Mr. Chadburne had at first been in conversation with the other men, but some pages of various hunting breeds attracted them and they were peering at pages over the shoulders of the ladies. Mamma and Mrs. Vandenhoff were engaged in motherly chatter until Mr. Vandenhoff was required to assist his wife in some recollections of the specific pattern for his mother's china back in New York. Mamma had a special place in her heart for such subjects, so she peppered the gentleman with question after question, keeping him occupied far longer than he clearly expected.

This left Mariah and Lord Dovington noticeably unattached. She tried not to appear nervous as he moved toward her. She was already nestled into a corner where she had gone to retrieve her mother's sewing basket so, unfortunately, there was little she could do to escape the man.

He loomed over her and she feverishly recited in her mind all her vows and grievances against him. They did little to counteract the effect of his dark, all-seeing eyes and the heat radiating from him. She tried to sit up very tall in the straight-backed chair she had chosen. No way was she going to let him see her as tiny and helpless. She should have selected a ladder, she supposed. The slow grin that spread over his face reminded her of an etching she'd seen depicting a tiger about to pounce on a helpless baby deer.

"You are not perusing the book of dogs," he noted. He voice was low and growling, as if his simple statement harbored some deeper, mysterious meaning.

"I've read it before."

"But apparently your curate has not. Pity he's left with the others to introduce him to it."

"I'm quite positive both my sister and Miss Vandenhoff are competent readers, sir."

"I'm sure they are. They appear competent at other things, as well. Aren't you concerned?"

"Concerned for what? It's not likely they'll build a fire on the book and catch the house ablaze."

"There are more destructive types of fire, Miss Langely, as I know for a fact you are well aware."

"Whatever are you talking about?"

It had probably been a bad idea to ask that. He leaned in closer to her and whispered. His words fell over her as tangibly as if he had touched her.

"Do not pretend you felt nothing in my arms today. You may deny for everyone else, but you can never deny it for me. I know the passion that burns in you, my dear. I just wonder if Mr. Skrewd knows of it, too."

Oh no! Why was he doing this? Did he fear she was not doing her best to help his cause? Or was he the tiger, indeed, toying with his pray simply for the sport of it? Either way, she refused to cower before him. They were not alone in some romantic setting where he could employ his schemes to entrap her. This was her house, her own mother was just steps away.

and she was not to be bullied by this man, no matter how foolish her actions had been today.

"What Mr. Skrewd does or does not know about me is hardly any of your concern," she snipped at him. "Don't you have your own business to attend?"

"You mean Miss Vandenhoff? You worry that I am not fawning over her or making cows eyes like some mutton-headed dolt?"

"I worry you are ignoring her and not attending her as a gentleman ought to attend a young lady who has captured his affections."

"Well, there's an easy answer for that, Miss Langley. You see, I have no affection at all for Miss Vandenhoff and I don't care that she knows it. I hate to tell you, but if you think I am here to snag her for myself, you are entirely mistaken."

"What? You don't intend to... but why then? Why have you brought them here?"

"For my cousin, of course. Look at him, he's doing his duty and making a fuss over the ladies, making nice that Miss Vandenhoff cannot possibly dismiss. He is the future of the Dovington title, Miss Langley. Not me."

"But *you* are the earl. Why would Miss Vandenhoff wish to marry your cousin if you have the title?"

She was more than confused now and it was quite a struggle to keep her voice low. No one seemed to have noticed them yet, and the earl reached to examine the embroidery she'd laid out on her lap. She knew he couldn't care less for her needle work, but it was good that he seemed to have some innocuous reason for his nearness to her just now.

"I intend never to marry," he said in a harsh whisper. "If you'd ever once met my father, you'd understand. I've nothing to give to my family tree but bitterness and failing, but I'm man enough to admit it. My father's line ends with me, and my cousin will be the one to carry it on. I'll do what I can to correct my father's mistakes, but once I'm gone it will be Ned to continue the name."

It took a few moments of silence for his words to sink into her brain and make sense. What on earth could she say after this revelation? It was stunning, to say the least. To think that this man should give up any hopes of a future just because of the hateful things his father had done... incomprehensible. She wished it did not sound so very gallant and noble to her.

"You should have told me whom I was supposed to be matching up, my lord."

"All I asked of you was to be a good hostess and to help Miss Vandenhoff appear at her best. You should not have presumed to know what I planned."

She couldn't resist forcing a smug grin for him. "But I did presume, sir, and it was exactly what you had planned, wasn't it? I simply guessed the wrong partner."

"So you did. And do you supposed you've guessed any better for yourself?"

"Excuse me?" She kept the smile on her face just in case someone might glance up from their current entertainments and wonder what they could possibly be discussing in such low, furtive tones.

"Your curate there. Are you so convinced that he'll marry you?'

Of all the nerve! Her heart thudded in her chest and her emotions warred. She didn't know if she felt fury that he would suggest she might not be good enough for Mr. Skrewd, or shame that what he suggested was true. She wasn't suitable for any decent gentleman's wife, not even the penniless curate. She was a bastard, and she'd proven today that the same wanton passion that had led to her unintentional existence ran unchecked in her blood.

The earl was correct. She could never marry anyone. It was a truth she had always known, always accepted. Why today it should suddenly hurt her so very badly she had no idea. Her eyes burned, but she glared at him all the same.

'What I do with Mr. Skrewd is my business and none of yours," she hissed out at him, still keeping that smile firmly in place. "Your business is to hire your nephew out for stud and then get yourself out of my house. All of you."

His eyes were fixed firmly on hers and he gave no indication at all that her words shocked or insulted him.

"It's *my* house, Miss Langley. I'll make myself at home here as long as I like."

"Then I suppose once things are settled with Miss Vandenhoff, I'll have to make sure you don't like."

He leaned even closer and his voice was barely audible now, but she heard him. She recognized the challenge.

"Don't play this game with me, Miss Langley. You showed your hand today, if you recall. There's very little you can do to me that I won't like, and very much I can do that you *will*."

His hand brushed over her cheek just enough to cause the temperature in the room to suddenly elevate. She knew he was right. Her threats were empty and there was very little she could do that might provide enough pressure or guilt or even discomfort to cause him to give up Renford Hall. She doubted any more positive form of influence would have any effect, either. A hundred secret kisses would never persuade him to leave them in peace, but it certainly would shatter hers forever. For all intents and purposes, her battle was already lost.

"You're certainly welcome to try, though," he added, finally backing away so that she could breathe freely again.

Once again she amazed him with her will and her unshrinking determination. He could see that his words stung her, but she would not back down. What sort of fiend was he that he felt so compelled to subdue her, to stand over her and make veiled threats and insinuations? He supposed he was just as he'd told her; he was his father's son and could hardly expect anything good of himself.

Here they were in polite company, surrounded by family and guests, and still he could barely restrain himself from sweeping her into his arms and taking up where the curate's dog had disrupted them earlier. She would hate him for it, of course, but he hardly cared about that. He'd tapped into an inferno inside of her and he knew he could do it again. In spite of herself, Miss Langley was a creature of passion and Dovington was not above using that against her.

Although why on earth would he? She knew the truth of his

schemes now and it was in her best interests to play along. She'd see that Ned and Miss Vandenhoff were put together as often as possible and if tonight's harmonious interplay was any indication, things were well on their way toward the goal. As Miss Langley had said, she wanted them out of her house. Dovington realized as well as she did that the best way to accomplish that was to bring those two together and rush them off to the altar.

There was no reason at all for Dovington to leer at her and torment her for her designs on the curate. They must be more than designs, too, given the pain he saw flash over her face when he questioned the man's intentions toward her. She must honestly care for him.

Only a beast would attack a lady on such a tender subject, and yet he had done so. It was all he could do right now not to attack her again, to remind her that by her very nature she had far more in common with a scoundrel like him than the righteous Mr. Skrewd. All it would take were a few kisses, some moments of burning caress, and she would be forced to admit the truth.

By God, he needed to get away from her. With his mind wandering in such ways, there was little he could do but ruin anything good that had begun to crop up around them. Acting on impulse he would scandalize his cousin, offend the Vandenhoffs, and ruin a woman who did not deserve to be ruined. Just as he'd always known, he was flawed to the core and there was no place for him in gentle society.

Tomorrow he would leave. Yes, he'd take himself away before he did anything more foolish and destructive than he already had. Miss Langley would continue her efforts to connect Ned with Miss Vandenhoff, and by the day of that silly ball they had planned, everything should fall into place.

As usual, everyone here would be much better off without him.

He cleared his throat and adjusted his coat as if suddenly bored with his gentlemanly perusal of the needlework he'd been pretending to admire. He stepped away from Miss Langley and her angry-sea eyes to speak loudly enough to be heard around the room.

"You have an excellent hand, Miss Langley. You should keep at that and it will be quite a showpiece when you are done. For me, however, I beg you excuse me. I must retire early as I intend to ride for Dovington Downs first thing in the morning."

"Dovington Downs, sir?" Mr. Vandenhoff asked from his seat near the ladies, probably thrilled for this interruption.

"Yes," the earl replied, moving away from Miss Langley as if he did not even recall she existed. "I have several pressing matters in the works and I dare not leave my steward alone for too long to manage them on his own. Oh, he's quite a competent man, but I cannot rest easy until these things are settled, you know."

"Indeed I do," Mr. Vandenhoff agreed. "Mrs. Vandenhoff chides me all the time, saying I work too hard and that I should have people do more of my things for me. We men of business know, though, don't we? If something is to be done right, we're going to have to do it ourselves."

"Er, exactly," Dovington replied, glancing at Miss Langley and pushing aside a wave of indecent thoughts regarding the various things that ought to be done to her.

Her eyes narrowed as if she could read his mind. "And when might we expect you to return, sir?"

"I should be back in three days."

Miss Renford looked up from her book and clapped her hands. "That means you'll return in time for our ball! You will be here for the ball, won't you?"

Where Miss Langley's blond hair was the color of heated gold, her younger sister's was pale like the petals of a spring flower. Almost-white ringlets framed her face and her huge blue eyes blinked up at him. The elder girl's gaze always seemed to burn with the heat of an erupting volcano, but this one waited for his answer like a frightened rabbit. He could hardly be short with her.

"I will be back in time for your ball, Miss Renford," he responded.

She was far more happy about that than she should have been, but he supposed she was young and naive and couldn't imagine that he might not be such a fine addition to their number as his title might imply. It had been so long since he was confronted with actual innocence and zeal that it made him feel very out of place, indeed.

"Well, then," Miss Langley said, as if speaking for the group. "I suppose we'll just have to find ways to entertain ourselves in your absence."

Damn it, but he had no doubt she would do just that and the very thought was like a cold, hard mass in his chest. He would be gone and things would carry on here just fine. Even better than with him present, perhaps. Hell, by the time he came back, maybe Miss Langely would have attached not only his cousin and the heiress, but herself and her curate, as well.

That was a thing, he realized, he was very happy not to be here to see.

Chapter 14

Moring arrived, finally, with gray skies and singing birds. Mariah welcomed it. She hadn't slept very well. Actually, she simply hadn't slept, at all.

Her mind had been tossed around by waves of emotion that, even all these hours later, she still couldn't quite understand. She hated that horrible earl. How dare he risk ruining her, kissing her as he had done and drawing from her things she hadn't even known she had held inside? Then he was spiteful enough to taunt her afterwards, reminding her who she was, what she was. He'd been right when he said she was unworthy, but she'd never forgive him for saying it.

But it hadn't been rage and unforgiveness that had kept her awake all through the night. It had been those lingering memories of his searing kiss, and then that cold, defeated shadow that had come over his eyes when he spoke of his father. She tried to tell herself she hadn't seen it, that it had meant nothing. But she knew she was wrong.

The earl thought himself even less worthy than he thought her. He had given up on any of the usual hopes and dreams of a man; he had everything, and yet he had nothing. He was just acting out his duty and waiting to die.

Try as she might, she couldn't hate him despite his cruel words, despite his reckless kisses and unrelenting selfishness. If not for her step-father who had given her a measure of respectability, for her mother who loved her unconditionally, and her sister who adored her—most of the time—she supposed she could be in the same dark place that he was. She could understand why he treated others with so little concern. He had no concern for himself.

And that, she knew, was tragic.

She still wanted him out of her house and far, far away from her life, but she just couldn't find it in herself to wish him evil. In fact, she had a ridiculous notion of what she could do to possible help the man. It was silly, of course, but maybe once this was done and he was off living his bleak, friendless life at his father's estate there was one little thing she could do to make him more human.

It was obvious what the man needed: *a puppy*.

She'd told Mr. Skrewd that she'd visit him today to make sure the puppy she selected for Ella was still the one that she wanted, and now she'd pick one out for the earl. She hoped there was still one available, actually. Hadn't the curate told her many of them were already spoken for? If she wanted to chose another, she'd best get herself over there.

With the sun just cresting the horizon and the sky a smear of milky golds and pinks, Mr. Skrewd would likely be preparing for morning prayer very soon. He might talk with some of the parishioners about the remaining puppies and perhaps even find takers for them all. If she was serious in her intent to gift one to the earl—and for some reason it seemed that she was—she'd best do so quickly.

It was an excellent excuse to give up on the tossing and turning. She leapt out of bed and selected clothing she could don without assistance. No doubt she looked less than ideal when, not fifteen minutes later, she dashed out one of the side doors and headed for the little hut with the faded red door that Mr. Skrewd called his home.

Her skirts sucked up the early dew and she shivered with chill, even as the sunlight grew brighter and morning mists began to clear around her. It dawned on her that this was a ridiculous, foolish errand and that she must need her head examined. Rushing out this early in the day in hopes of securing a puppy, of all things, for the horrible Earl of Dovington who seemed to care nothing for her but to make her life miserable? There was no reason to it.

Perhaps she merely wanted an excuse to visit the puppies. No one could tell her *that* wasn't a perfectly reasonable goal.

Who wouldn't go out early to enjoy the delights of wagging tails and fat, furry bellies? Puppies were nothing less than a gift from God and the fact that she wanted to share one of them with the hard-hearted earl simply meant she was a decent, Christian soul.

The sun was a low golden orb just over the horizon now and Dovington squinted into it. He'd not had much sleep and even in the mist-blurred light of morning, it was too bright for him. He didn't like waiting, but there was nothing to do as his carriage was being readied. He was glad to be leaving before any of the family were up; the last thing he needed was to run into Miss Langley again. Clearly he could not be trusted around that woman.

From the corner of his eye he noticed a dog. The curate's dog, if he was correct. What the devil was that thing doing here at this hour? She disappeared around the far corner of the house, so he followed.

A pathway ran along there, through a dense thicket of lilac that nearly overwhelmed him with its fresh, heady scent, and then on behind several other garden areas. The path meandered away from the house and up toward a tree-covered hillside. There was that little hut, the old gamekeeper's hut, Miss Langley had called it. Oddly enough, the dog went to the hut and scratched at the door.

Miss Langley said they had a lodger there, did she? Well, whoever it was must give out scraps to the neighborhood dogs. Rather a quaint picture, in fact. He almost smiled with some misplaced sense of nostalgia.

But then the door opened and he could see just who this scrap-feeding lodger was.

Mr. Ben Skrewd. Indeed, the curate himself.

He lived here? Why should a respectable curate live in something like a hermit's hut behind the home of a widow with two very pretty daughters? Having a house readied in the village, Miss Langley had said. Hell, Dovington could think of any number of reasons the curate might wish those preparations to dawdle.

And just what did Miss Langley think of this? She probably loved it, having her admirer so close at hand. Did she think he would marry her and give her a fine place in her little society?

She hardly needed a husband for that. She'd obviously done very well for herself, taking over after her step-father's death and clearly making herself a valued and respected member of this community. Dovington should never have used the accident of her birth to tease her. She was every bit the lady and he'd been wrong to suggest otherwise.

His self-chastisement ceased immediately, though, when the weathered red door opened wider and Dovington realized Mr. Skrewd wasn't alone. Miss Langley was with him.

Dovington could see them clearly, though it was obvious they were too deep in conversation to glance over his way. He ground his teeth, freezing behind a screen of greenery, waiting to make sure his eyes weren't deceiving.

By God, the two of them were in that tiny hut, and the curate wasn't simply giving spiritual comfort. By the contented smile on Miss Langley's face, it appeared the type of comfort the curate had been offering was just what she had come for.

But at this ungodly hour of the day? The sun was barely up. What on earth could the chit be thinking, to show up here now? Dovington had seen no signs of her inside the house, so how had she come to be out here already?

His blood raced hot. Not *already*. Perhaps the word he ought to use for her presence behind that red door was *still*. There was one glaringly obvious reason why he might not have seen her in her own home this morning: she quite possibly had been out here in this hut *all night*!

He balled his fists and considered marching over to Mr. Skrewd and planting a facer that would allow the good reverend to present his morning homily right at the very gates of St. Peter. He held himself back, though.

What was it to him if Miss Langley chose to ruin herself this way? She was nothing to him. No, she was less than nothing. She was a nuisance and an annoyance. He could not be happier if she found some man to take her and get her out of his hair.

Hell, instead of pummeling the man, he ought to go up to

Skrewd and shake his damn hand. So Miss Langley thought she could get herself a husband by playing fast with the lowly curate? Well, that was perfectly fine. Let her. She could marry the man, raise ten screaming brats in whatever village would have them, and be out of The Grove.

Unless, of course, the curate was simply taking advantage of the situation. Did he realize his little ladybird would not bring the house and the lands into their union? As that bit of information had come as a surprise to Miss Langley, perhaps their neighbors had not been made fully aware of things, either. It was entirely possible Mr. Skrewd saw in Miss Langley a charming addition to his bed *and* an easy escape from his hut.

Dovington was back to considering fisticuffs again. No, he would not. He did not care what Miss Langley did. If she had made her own bed with Mr. Skrewd, it was her lot to lie in it. No matter how much better she might look nestled into the over-large master suit at Dovington Downs.

Hell and damnation, he would not let his mind wander there.

He was leaving this place. His carriage was being brought round even now, his horses were rested, and there was nothing holding him back.

Certainly not Miss Langely. She and Mr. Skrewd seemed perfectly content in that faded doorway of that little hut. Anyone but Dovington would count them a lovely couple and wish them well.

Dovington wished them to the devil. While he was at it, he wished himself there, too. Maybe an eternity tormented by demons would make him forget how Miss Langley had felt in his arms or how the pain nearly radiated from her when he insulted her last night.

Indeed, she was much better off with her curate than she could ever be with someone like him.

Chapter 15

Mariah's head was swimming. Their ball was this evening and she'd been consumed by preparations the full past three days. Dinner was already over for their usual house party, now guests for the ball would be arriving soon. Still, her list of things to get done did not seem to be growing any shorter. Whose foolish notion had it been to attempt this sort of thing, anyway? It should have taken a month to prepare for a proper ball, not the mere three days she'd been allowed.

And where was that dratted earl? He'd said he'd be back in time for the ball. Not that she cared one way or another, but he'd promised Ella and it would be in very poor form to let the girl down. This was the first ball they'd ever hosted and even though Ella was not officially out yet, Mamma had decided there could be nothing wrong with allowing her to participate in the country dances here in their own home. Ella wanted to be able to say she'd had an earl in attendance at her first ball. If Dovington knew what was good for him, he'd turn up in time.

Besides, Mariah had asked Mr. Skrewd to hold back two puppies, and only one of them was supposed to remain here. Dovington had better show up and be happy with his puppy. If she had to keep it she'd find herself adoring it and feeding it and scratching it softly behind the ears and thinking of that dratted, vile man every time she did so.

That was why she found herself watching out windows all day. *That* was why she asked the servants if they'd seen him over and over all day. She wanted to finish their business and be done with the man.

The past days had been very busy making plans for the ball. She'd taken great care, though, so make sure there was ample time for Mr. Chadburne to be in company with Miss Vandenhoff. Ella had been a great help in that area, coming up with entertainments for them all even if Mariah had been too busy with arrangements to participate with them. Mr. Skrewd had also been a great asset, joining in on those entertainments and making up for Mariah's absence. She would have to thank him tonight for so generously giving his time while she was unavailable.

She and Mamma had invited a few others of their closest acquaintances so hopefully the atmosphere would be friendly and festive. Miss Vandenhoff had seemed to get better with every passing day and by tonight Mariah had every reason to expect the girl might be not merely tolerable, but actually pleasant. There was no doubt that the earl—if he did ever deign to show up—would be satisfied with her efforts.

What better place to announce a betrothal than here at a ball amongst friends? Mariah was taking extra care that everything would be just perfect. Miss Vandenhoff would have this night to remember forever and Mariah was determined that it should be a happy memory. Perhaps that union had been devised by others, but there was no reason for the couple not to find themselves happy in it.

"Are you happy with your selection?"

Mariah jumped. She'd been alone in the corridor, pausing yet again to glance out the window at the still empty yard in front of the house, and had not expected Mr. Skrewd to be in this part of the house. But here he was.

"I... my selection?"

"The puppies," he explained. "Have you been to check on them again?"

"Yes, I was out there. They certainly are a handful. I don't know how you've managed, so many bounding pups in your little hut out back."

"Indeed, it has been rather chaotic ," Mr. Skrewd replied with a smile. "Still, it will seem awfully quiet once they are all gone."

"You've found homes for all of them, then?"

"I have, although one of those homes is with me. I decided

Bess ought to be allowed the company of one of her pups after all this."

"You have a soft heart, sir. Take care no one learns of it or you'll soon find every needy dog dumped at your doorstep."

"Lord, I might never be out of your gracious lodgings here then. Who else would rent room to a man with more dogs than he has sense?"

"I'm sure many people would have great respect for it. So were you on your way back out to them now? You wish to say good-bye again?"

"Er, yes, I'm afraid so. Those little beasties have certainly grown on me."

"I understand. The back door of this wing is still unlocked, so you should be able to go out and then let yourself back in again."

"Thank you. I hope that—"

But his hopes were interrupted when her mother appeared around the corner, coming from the main part of the house. She smiled when she saw Mariah and gave a friendly nod to Mr. Skrewd.

"Ah, here you are. What are you up to, hiding back here?'

Mr. Skrewd seemed decidedly uncomfortable, but Mariah knew her mother was simply teasing them. She knew all about the puppy surprise for Ella and it must come as no shock to see Mariah conspiring in a corridor with the owner of said puppies.

"I'm sorry, ma'am, I was simply going to—" Mr. Skrewd began nervously.

Mamma waved her hand at him. "You were talking about Ella's puppy. Yes, I know all about Mariah's big surprise for her sister. Thank you so much, Mr. Skrewd, for helping us give something to Ella that will mean so very much to her."

"Indeed, it is my pleasure, Mrs. Renford. And thank you for taking the little, er, angel off my hands."

"I'm sure your hands have been very full, Mr. Skrewd. I think it's lovely, though, that we can include so many wonderful things in our little impromptu ball this evening. A new pet for Ella, and an engagement being announced... what a remarkable evening it will be."

"An engagement, ma'am?" he asked.

Mamma pursed her lips and looked chagrined. "Heavens, was I not supposed to mention anything about that?"

"I don't think we are to speak of it just yet, Mamma, but of course Mr. Skrewd can know. He can certainly be trusted with Miss Vandenhoff's secret."

The poor man appeared as if he were not so sure that he could be trusted. "What is this? Miss Vandenhoff's secret?"

"Oh, it's hardly a secret, really. Surely you've noticed these past few days," Mariah said with a coy little grin. "Miss Vandenhoff and Mr. Chadburne have been quite inseparable, haven't they? Oh, don't pretend to be surprised. It isn't the first time a wealthy merchant family has sought to improve their connections by introducing their daughter to a gentleman of high standing."

"But... Miss Vandenhoff and Mr. Chadburne?"

The curate seemed to have had no clue at all about this. Silly man. He was really going to have to learn to be more observant.

"It is why they are here, after all," Mariah explained. "The earl and Mr. Vandenhoff have some sort of understanding, apparently, and this has been pre-arranged."

"You can't really believe so? Surely not, Miss Langley. If Mr. Vandenhoff was so heartless to insist on matching his daughter with someone so clearly not of her choosing, why on earth would he select Chadburne and not the earl himself?"

"Mr. Chadburne is the earl's heir," Mariah said. "He is a fine gentleman. I've seen for myself how attentive he's been, showing himself to be everything charming and noble. Perhaps Miss Vandenhoff was not the one to first have the notion of finding a husband during her stay, but you must acknowledge that her demeanor has shown great improvement as the days have ticked by."

"Yes, but that is only due to... that is, you think that is because she is coming to love Mr. Chadburne?"

Mamma gave a matronly chuckle. "That is one of the main causes for improvement in a young lady's demeanor. I believe Mariah has done an excellent job arranging things. By the end of the ball tonight, I expect there will be no doubt in anyone's mind that Mr. Chadburne and Miss Vandenhoff are fully committed."

The subject seemed to very nearly terrify Mr. Skrewd. Mariah found his sudden pallor and school-boy stammering quite amusing. She'd never known he was so anxious. But after all, he was rather young.

Perhaps the idea of marriage was still a frightening thing for him. Mariah could hardly blame him. It must be uncomfortable to have Mamma rattling on about it this way. Besides, the couple in question were little more than strangers to them. It did seem a bit impertinent to be discussing such intimate details of their lives this way.

"It will all work out, Mr. Skrewd," Mariah said, helping him escape this conversation. "Now, why don't you go see to the puppies while we go see that everything is in place for the ball."

"The guests from the village will be arriving any time now," Mamma said. "And I was looking for you to help me with a few details, Mariah."

"Of course, Mamma."

"I'll leave you to your work then," Mr. Skrewd said, obviously eager to get away.

He mumbled some gracious thanks and then hurried down the corridor toward the back doorway that would open onto the path closest to his little hut. Mariah took her mother's arm and led the way back toward the lighted rooms with all the bustling servants and loudly tuning musicians.

"Very well, Mamma, tell me what is still needed to be ready."

"Well, I was wanting to ask your opinion on the number of windows we have left open tonight, but now I feel awful about interrupting. You and Mr. Skrewd seemed quite sociable there in the darkened corridor."

"Mamma, please. I've asked you to leave that subject alone."

"And I do try, my dear, but you can't blame a woman for noticing. You've spent considerable time with him of late, haven't you? No, don't deny it, I know you've gone to his house more than was strictly necessary."

"You read too much into things, Mamma!"

"Do I? Or do I have reason to hope for not one, but two

117

engagements to be announced by the end of this evening?"

"Heavens, Mamma! Now you're embarrassing me."

"But dearest, you know that I'm not blind. The man has been more cheerful than usual lately, and he's made every excuse possible to show up here each day. Oh, very well, if you insist I'll stop speaking of it. But I won't be one bit surprised when I learn you've given up your foolish intent to stay single."

Mariah gritted her teeth. There was no use arguing the point. Mamma was determined to cling to this notion of hers and it would only upset her to persist in denying things now. Once the ball was over and she could see for herself that there was nothing between her and Mr. Skrewd besides a few pleasantries and a concern for the puppies, then perhaps she could listen to reason.

She would be disappointed, of course, but that would likely be tempered by the announcement that Mr. Chadburne and Miss Vandenhoff were to be wed. When the earl invited them all to remove to Dovington Downs to prepare for the nuptials, then Mamma would forget all about her silly designs on Mr. Skrewd. She would have her home back, and they could once again focus on preparing for Ella's come-out next year.

Of course, all that would depend on the earl's actual presence at the ball tonight, wouldn't it? Without him here to remove everyone to his estate the engagement would simply mean they'd be stuck with these houseguests a while longer and would be subjected to additional mooning and cows eyes all day long.

Drat that earl. Where on earth could he be and why wasn't he here as he promised he would be?

The earl was concealed in the dim recess of a doorway. He held his breath as Miss Langley and her mother walked by. He heard their voices go round the next corner as he ground his teeth.

So, Mrs. Renford knew of her daughter's secret visits to Mr. Skrewd's house, did she? And she expected an engagement. Of course, Dovington should not be surprised by any of this. He'd seen the pair of them in the doorway of Skrewd's hut three days ago. He knew the passions inside Miss Langley, and he had eyes to see what any other man might see in her. Of course the curate would want her.

Dovington had been an absolute idiot to have come back here hoping for something else.

Damn, when would he ever learn? He knew the truth about himself. How could he have been so ready to forget it all simply because his steward back at his estate had given him hopeful news? There was no hope where he was concerned.

So what if he had made farther strides than expected, paying off debts that he'd not been expected to pay for another two years? His house was still crumbling, needing far more than his pitiful reconstruction projects had been able to accomplish thus far. His tenants still lived in near poverty, his lands still lay fallow and unproductive. Had he really allowed himself to think—to dream—that perhaps he might consider a future for himself?

It was laughable. His estate was in tatters and Miss Langley was off limits to him. Period. No matter how encouraging his steward had been about what he'd called "miraculous headway," nothing could change the fact of reality. All of Dovington's work now was to pay off in the future for Ned and his bride. Dovington had no right to hope for himself.

He waited until the voices and footsteps had faded into the distance then left the corridor. His task here was nearly done and soon he'd have no reason to remain. He'd put Miss Langley out of his mind and do what needed to be done.

He'd hunt down his cousin for an update.

It wasn't much of a hunt, really. He found Ned helping arrange flowers in baskets dotting the large room the family had designated for their ballroom tonight. Miss Renford was cooing over the sagging bouquet Ned had put together and the small group of musicians at the far end of the room were talking amongst themselves and idly tuning their instruments. Miss Renford was the first to notice Dovington's arrival and she jumped when he made his way to them.

"Good evening, Miss Renford, Ned," he said with a polite bow.

"So you did turn up again!" Ned chided with a grin. "We

were beginning to think you'd abandoned us."

"I promised Miss Renford I'd return for her ball, and here I am. I apologize for missing dinner, but I was delayed."

"I can have the kitchen put together a tray for you, sir," Miss Renford said in her delicate little voice.

"No, I ate on the road, but thank you. I would not wish to trouble anyone just now. I see all is in readiness for tonight's event."

"Doesn't the room look lovely? I don't even remember the last time we hosted anything here," Miss Renford said, beaming at the glowing lamps and the careful decorations. "It took six men to carry the carpet when they rolled it up yesterday."

"It is a most excellent room and I'm sure the grand Renford ball will be hailed as a riotous success," the earl replied. "But I wonder if you can spare my cousin just now, Miss Renford? I should very much like a word with him, please."

"Of course, sir," she said, curtsying and giving both of them a weak little smile. "I'll see if my mother requires anything else."

She scurried away and Dovington watched after her. "Like a scared rabbit, that one is."

"You do tend to be a bit overwhelming, cousin."

"So they tell me."

"But what do you wish to say to me?" Ned asked. "Perhaps we should retire to somewhere a bit more private."

"Indeed."

Clearly Ned knew exactly what the topic for their discussion should be. Good. That meant he was prepared. Things had gone just as planned and Ned had done everything needed to see that Miss Vandenhoff would accept his proposal. Dovington could be done with this place—and the whole Renford family—by morning.

They left the ballroom and Dovington led the way to the study. It was unoccupied and he took the light from the corridor to find his way lighting the lamp at the desk. The heavy drapes were drawn, keeping out whatever rays of sunset might still be trying to filter in, and the lamp cast dancing shadows around the room. They made the expression on Ned's face unreadable as Dovington poured his cousin a drink.

"You have been often in company with Miss Vandenhoff while I've been absent?" he asked.

"Yes," Ned replied. "The younger set has done much to pass the time enjoyably."

"And you have found the time enjoyable? And the company?"

"Er, yes, actually. I've been quite happy with my stay here at Renford Hall."

He didn't bother to correct the misnomer. What did he care what Ned called the place? The important thing was that this house and its lands were productive and Dovington could use all of it to satisfy his father's debt.

"I am happy to hear it. Shall I assume you've had opportunity to speak with Mr. Vandenhoff, then?"

Ned became decidedly uncomfortable. "Well... you see, that's been a bit of a problem. I haven't quite gotten around to that."

It figured. Dovington couldn't be angry about it, though. Ned was young, and speaking to a young lady's father might be quite a daunting task. It was understandable that Ned had preferred to wait until his cousin returned.

"No matter. I'll speak to him for you and get everything settled."

'No! I mean... I hope you will let me deal with this in my own way."

"Your own way? You have some special plan in your mind?"

"Yes, actually, I do. I just... this is a delicate matter, as you can understand. Please let me handle things tonight."

"Very well. Since you are convinced all is going positively, I suppose you can be trusted to work things out for yourself."

"Thank you, cousin. I hope I don't disappoint."

"I'm sure that you won't. You've proved to be one of the few bright spots in the Chadburne line, so I look forward to letting you lead."

That notion seemed to make Ned just a bit nauseous, so Dovington clapped him on the back. Ned choked on his drink.

"There, there, lad. It's only matrimony, after all. You'll do fine, and I wish you much happiness."

"Do you, cousin? Do you truly?"

"Of course I do."

The words came almost too easily, but Dovington realized he honestly meant them. Whatever true happiness was, he did wish it for Ned. It was about time someone in the Chadburne line found it for himself.

"Then... perhaps I ought to go see to a few things before all the guests are arrived."

Dovington nodded. "Yes, you go do that. You can report to me later."

"Yes. Later. Right."

Poor Ned. Already his nerves were a mess, Dovington could tell. The younger man downed that last of his drink in one wincing gulp, and his hand noticeably shook as he deposited his glass on the tray. But he got up from his chair, adjusted his coat, and headed off to the war. At least, that's what his expression said as he marched out of the study.

Dovington shook his head, but smiled. Ned was a good lad and he was proud of him, standing up and taking the reins on his own. Mr. Vandenhoff would be impressed. Tomorrow morning Dovington would confer with them and they'd put some things in writing. The betrothal would be official and Vandenhoff money could begin flowing his way. Everything was made even sweeter by the knowledge that Ned might actually be content with his bride.

As Mr. Skrewd, no doubt, would be with his. Everything was working out into a nice, tidy package, wasn't it? He ought to be quite pleased with himself. Instead he felt cold and empty inside. He knew what to do, though. He'd seen his father fill that void hundreds of times.

He topped-off his glass and decided to get staggering drunk.

Chapter 16

Everything was going remarkably well. Mariah glanced around the gaily lit room and smiled at the fruits of her efforts. Mamma was smiling and showing the carefully placed flower arrangements to Mrs. Wakefield, while Mr. and Mrs. Benson were making the acquaintance of the Vandenhoff's. The two young Smith sisters were making eyes at the Martin brothers across the room, while Mr. Chadburne and Mr. Skrewd were making themselves comfortable at the punch bowl. The musicians played lightly, preparing for the first dance that would be gathering soon. Their first Renford ball would be in full bloom and Ella appeared to be nearly floating as she grinned up at her sister.

"Isn't it heavenly?"

"It's beautiful," Mariah agreed. "Thank you for your help with it. I think we can all count on a most pleasant evening tonight."

"I hope so! It's so very important that all will be well."

"Don't worry, I'm sure that it will be. I'm only sorry, for your sake, that the earl did not return in time to make an appearance."

"Oh, he's arrived back some time ago," Ella said, then wrinkled her brow. "I can't imagine why we haven't seen him here yet. He must still be refreshing himself after his travel."

"He's here? In this house?"

"Yes. I saw him an hour ago. He assured me he'd be in attendance."

So the blackguard returned and had promised her sister—again—that he'd attend and still he was not here? The nerve of him! She'd have to find him immediately and tell him just what she thought of such behavior. How dare he disappoint Ella this way.

"If he is here, then I should go find him."

"Find him? Why?" Ella asked.

"To box his ears, of course. He promised he'd be here and I won't have him letting you down."

"Letting me down? I'm fine, Mariah, truly. It makes no real difference to me if he attends."

"Don't be silly. You wanted an earl at your first ball, and by heaven you shall have one. Keep an eye on things and I'm going to hunt the man down. Take extra care to make sure Miss Vandenhoff enjoys her time here tonight, will you?"

Ella frowned and glanced around the room. "Very well but... I'm not certain where she is just now."

"She's here somewhere, I talked to her a few moments ago. I'm sure she'll turn up as soon as the dancing begins."

"I hope so," Ella sighed.

"She will. This ball is truly about her, as you well know."

Ella didn't seem especially pleased to be reminded of that. "Yes, yes. I know."

"But of course it is yours, as well. Enjoy yourself, Ella. I shall be right back."

Ella nodded and Mariah left her there to go and locate the absentee earl. When she found him, he would certainly hear about his behavior. Such rudeness!

She asked a footman in the corridor if he knew where the earl was and he seemed to think he'd seen him in the direction of the study. That made sense. Step-Papa had kept his spirits there, so of course that's where she might find the earl. She drew back her shoulders and headed up the corridor toward the back of the house.

Light was spilling out from the doorway as she approached, so she knew she had found him. He was, indeed, in the study. He wasn't at the desk, though, or sitting in one of the comfortable leather chairs. It took her eyes a moment to find him, the dim lamplight making eerie shapes against the walls.

He was sitting the window. It was open and a chilly breeze blew in, adding to the flickering effect from the lamps. She could not make out his expression, but she could feel his eyes on her as she stepped in through the doorway. She wasn't sure what she'd expected him to be doing here, but sitting amongst half a dozen empty decanters seemed to be a bit excessive, even for him.

Now she could see him smile, his teeth showing as if in a snarl. One decanter still held liquid, but he was rapidly altering that. The breeze slightly redirected the stream as the contents were poured out the window, little droplets splashing here and there as they went down into the shrubbery below.

"What are you doing? That's my step-father's best whiskey!" she exclaimed.

"Not anymore."

"And the brandy, and the Madeira... you've dumped it all out the *window*?"

'Not all of it," he replied. "I started out drinking it, then realized what vile, ruinous stuff it is. After that I've been dumping it out the window."

'But... that's insane."

"No, wasting a life wallowing in this swill the way my father did was insane. You've surely no great love for it, Miss Langley. Or do you creep down here unseen and sample the stock?"

"Of course not. I just can't imagine... you've truly emptied all of those out the window?"

"Would you prefer I poured them onto the carpets?"

"Don't be ridiculous. I was here to chastise you for ignoring our ball, but now I'm not sure that I want you there. You likely smell of alcohol and will very possibly fall over should you try to stand up and dance."

"I'm not drunk, my dear. And I'm flattered that you should wish to dance with me."

"I never said that!" she declared. "I've no inclination at all to dance with you, my lord."

"No, I suppose not. You'll be too busy with your curate, at any rate."

"Are you back on that topic? I should have thought after three days you'd forget all about it."

He dropped the decanter onto the sill with the others and rose up swiftly, standing tall and steady and making her wish she had not come quite this close to him. Although, truth be told, as

125

her gaze took in his full form and she struggled again to meet his dark, probing eyes, a big part of her wished to move even closer. Much too close, in fact.

He'd removed his coat so she'd found him in his shirtsleeves. They were rumpled and rolled, showing the strong tendons of his arms and proving that he'd not relied on padding to make his shoulders appear so broad and so masterful. She seemed very small, indeed, standing next to him, though by all accounts she was not a petite female. Perhaps it was the way he was glaring at her, or perhaps it was the persistent memory of how she'd felt in his arms that day on the ridge... she had no way to say, but the feeling of vulnerability only grew as he took another step nearer.

"I've forgotten nothing, Miss Langley. I wonder if you have?"

She took a step away, but he followed, looming over her. "I... I think we should go down to the ball, sir. People are expecting you."

"No one cares whether I am there or not. *You're* the one who came looking for me, Miss Langley."

"Because you promised my sister. Surely your cousin wishes you to be there for his happy announcement."

He growled at her. "That damned announcement. Yes, after tonight everyone will be so very happy, won't they? What of you and your curate? Do you expect some sort of announcement?"

"Can you not stop teasing me with that? What is this fascination you have for Mr. Skrewd, anyway?"

"Mine? I have none, believe me. It is yours that I'm questioning."

"Well, you should stop. I've heard enough about Mr. Skrewd from you, sir. You've no reason to talk that way about him."

"Then how should I talk about him?" he asked, still moving toward her so that she was forced to take another step back. "Should I mention that when he marries you he'll be taking a woman who so easily throws herself into the arms of other men when he's not looking?"

Drat, but she was up against the desk now; she could back away no further. Still the earl moved toward her, his eyes fixed on hers with that familiar fire burning behind them. She tried desperately to quench the answering heat that rose up inside her.

"I do not throw myself. That was not throwing."

"Well it certainly wasn't crying out in demure resistance," he said.

"Whatever it was, it's ungentlemanly of you to bring it up," she snapped. "Now if you truly aren't jug-bit to the point of falling over, perhaps you will put yourself together and come down to the ball."

"Because you wish to dance with me?"

"No! Because you promised my sister you'd be there."

"And what have you promised your curate?"

He wasn't letting up. He was inching ever closer, nearly touching her now and there was nowhere for her to go. Why must he do this to her? What satisfaction could he possibly get from tormenting her this way, waving her own failings in her face and reminding her that no decent man could ever truly want her? She wished he really was drunk so at least she could blame the spirits for his actions, but she could not.

"Why do you persist in this?" she asked, her voice coming out tight and unsure. "Things have been going so well here while you were gone. I had thought... I hoped when you returned we could at least be friends, you and I."

"Friends? You want to be friends with me, Miss Langley?"

He glared at her, his eyes searching hers and boring through the calm, unfeeling facade she was desperate to maintain. His gaze held her long after she gave him a feeble nod of agreement.

"Yes, sir. I want to be friends."

He lurched out and grasped her shoulders, forcing her to stare up at him. She dared not even blink.

"No, Miss Langley. I'm afraid I can't do that. We can never be friends."

She wished she wasn't so saddened to hear those words. But then she wished she wasn't quite so thrilled when he pulled her tightly against himself and leaned in to kiss her again. Oh heavens, but it was even more delightful a second time! Now she knew what to do, and her body responded in an instant.

Without the bulk of his coat, the warmth coming off of him soaked into her skin right away. When she wrapped her arms around him she could feel the contours of his solid form, the muscles and sinews that gave him that remarkable, manly shape. If he felt this much better to her fingertips with just one layer of linen shirt, how wonderful he would feel with nothing between them!

Her body burned at the thought of it and she pressed herself closer against him. His lips covered hers, nibbled her, and drew such sensation that she sighed involuntarily. He replied with a growl, the sound of a beast claiming its prize, intending never to give it up.

But he would give her up. He'd made that clear from the start, hadn't he? This was nothing more than entertainment from him. She had to remember that, no matter how earth shattering it was for her.

His earth would not shatter. She could kiss him over and over and he wouldn't care. Not only was he opposed to the notion of a commitment, he'd announced they couldn't even be friends. She was kissing him as if he provided her life itself, yet she knew he wouldn't hesitate to walk away and watch part of her die.

How could she allow herself to be tormented this way? She couldn't. She deserved more than fleeting pleasure and long lasting pain. The earl had dragged her heart to the edge and she had to defend herself before she tumbled over. Forever.

She pushed him away.

"No! Stop this; we cannot, my lord."

He did not quite release her. "I assure you, my dear, we most certainly can."

"Well, *I* cannot. Take your hands off me. Now."

He did, complimenting the action with one blessed step away from her. At last, she could breathe and her head was finally clearing. She had to get away from him before his magic began to work on her all over again. She'd be lost at that point.

"I... I have to go."

He didn't stop her. She slid away from him then practically dashed out the door. Her heart pounded in her chest and her cheeks felt as if they would burst into flame. She couldn't go back to the ball, not now when everyone might see how distraught she must be.

She knew where to go. She knew what might possibly help soothe the ruin she felt, the ache of a heart she could no longer protect. It was too late for that, she realized now. There was nothing anyone could do to save a heart that was already broken.

Chapter 17

He stared after her. She'd literally run from him, so eager to be away from his touch. He couldn't really blame her, either. He'd run from himself if he thought it would do any good.

He turned back to the window and grabbed up one of the decanters. Damn, what an idiot notion to dump it all out. He smashed the decanter against the far wall. The sound was only temporarily satisfying. Once all the little shards had settled, he was still alone with himself in the silence.

Alone. The way he'd been for so long and the way he had planned to remain. It was an unbearable thought now. Mariah Langley had shined some kind of light into his dark corners and he was not content to retreat to them again.

But what could he do? She'd rejected him and she'd left. Definitively.

Well, she'd left. She'd not truly rejected him, since all he'd really offered her were insults and ruin. It was unreasonable to expect anyone *not* to reject such things. He could never fault her for being unreasonable.

Damn it all, but he could not fault her for anything. She knew nothing of him but that he was self-centered, rude, and a derelict. What on earth was there in that to recommend him? Nothing, save his ridiculous title.

But that did count for something, didn't it? True, he never expected to share it with anyone, but what if he did? No matter how worthless he was, that title meant something. His wife would enjoy the benefits of it; she'd be a countess, mother to noble-born children and respected everywhere she might go.

Would that be of interest to Miss Langley? As much as he hated the fact of his parentage, it suddenly dawned on him that because of it she might see beyond his many obvious failings. Was there even the slightest chance that she'd be willing to trade in her status as the bastard child of no one for the decorum that came with bearing a title? *His* title?

For so many years he'd refused to let himself contemplate such a thing, but right now it seemed there was nothing else he could think of. He could offer his title to Miss Langley and she might even consider it. He could offer her legitimacy, and he could promise to care for her mother and sister. Yes, that might just motivate her. She might decide that she wanted a title, after all. In the process, then, she'd have to take him with it.

That is, unless she accepted the bloody little curate first.

Well, he'd simply not let that happen. If he was going to live his life pining away like this, he sure as hell wanted to know he'd done all that he could. If she was truly to be rid of him, he'd make sure she had to reject an honest to God decent proposal.

He grabbed up his coat and stormed out into the darkened corridor, his footsteps echoing until they were drowned out by the sounds of music and laughter as he approached the ballroom. The footman cowered as he swept into the room, searching the small crowd for Miss Langley's form. The shimmering peach colored gown she'd been wearing would show her to excellent effect in the gleaming light here. He watched the dancers, examined the few ladies sitting in chairs, and it was obvious she wasn't here.

"So you are here, my lord," Mrs. Renford said cheerfully as she came up to greet him. "I'm happy to see you've returned."

He couldn't be bothered with pleasantry just now. Only one thing mattered and he needed to find her.

"Where is Miss Langley?"

"Mariah? Well, I have no idea. She was here a few moments ago. Perhaps she has gone to confer with the servants on some matter or other."

A nauseating thought entered his mind. *Skrewd.* Where was Mr. Skrewd?

Nowhere, it seemed. The room was as vacant of him as it was of Miss Langley. The blood in Dovington's veins turned cold. *She'd gone off with her lover. He was too late.*

But he knew where they'd go. Only one place made sense. With everyone here in the house enjoying the ball, it would be easy for the couple to steal away for some private moments outside. In that damn hut.

"Excuse me, ma'am," he said, barely recalling propriety and giving her the requisite bow. "I must tend to something."

Someone else tried to speak with him, but he paid no mind. He caught a brief glimpse of Ned off in the corner with Miss Renford, but he didn't bother to acknowledge their existence. There'd be plenty of time to greet Ned and to tell Miss Renford she was the prettiest belle at her very first ball. For now, he was storming back out of the ballroom.

Back to the darkened corridor, past the study and toward the turn at the far end. Beyond that, he found the narrow door that led out to the garden, the side garden that was little in use and overflowing with lilacs. He followed the path until he could see the outline of the hill where the little hut was. Sure enough, he could make out a faint light in the window. The hut was not empty. Shadows darkened the window and as he approached, he heard the unmistakable sound of laughter.

He knew nothing of the last few steps he took. All he was aware of was the urgency, the need to get himself in through that red door as quickly as possible. He had to stop them, no matter what they were up to.

The door banged open, dishes rattled on a nearby shelf from the force of it. Dovington ducked his head and peered in. One dim taper flickered on the table, the light spilling over the cramped room. His eyes adjusted readily.

There she was. Just as expected, his eyes fell on her and she was not alone. She was sprawled on the floor, her gown rumpled carelessly and her arms wrapped tightly around... a puppy?

"What the devil...?"

She sat up quickly and tucked her ankles carefully under her skirts, patting her hair and pushing the puppy off of her before it upset the already daringly low cut of her gown. Another puppy took its place, dancing on her and wrestling with its partner. A third appeared then, clambering over the others and flopping its soggy pink tongue. Miss Langley, however, looked past the wriggling little masses of black and white fur and glared up at him.

"What are *you* doing here?"

"I should ask you the same."

"As if it's any of your business what I'm doing here."

"Of course it's my business. This is my property and I'll not have you bring shame on it, rollicking on the floor of a bachelor's house!"

"I am rollicking with puppies, sir. You find that particularly shameful?"

"Of course not, but... where is Mr. Skrewd?"

"Dancing at the ball, I presume."

"Then why did you come here?"

"For the puppies. I thought they might... well, I am looking after them, that's all."

"And why should you be looking after Mr. Skrewd's puppies?"

"Because they are not all Mr. Skrewd's puppies. These two are spoken for. I've selected them for..."

She didn't finish, though he gave her ample time. "For whom?"

"One is for Ella. I was going to surprise her after the ball."

"I see. And the other?"

"It's for... someone else."

"And I want to know whom."

"It doesn't matter. I doubt he really wants it, anyway."

He? By God, she had another man to be giving gifts to? He'd throttle the man, whoever he was.

"Who, damn it? Give me his name."

She thought long and hard before answering. When she finally did, she fairly spat the word at him.

"You."

"Me?"

"Yes, *you*. I thought you might... it doesn't matter now."

"It does matter! Why on earth did you think you needed to give me a puppy?"

"Because you were sad. It's idiotic, I know, but when you left three days ago you seemed so defeated by everything your

134

father did to you, how he left you... I just thought that perhaps if you had someone—something—who cared about you... well, I thought you might want something like that. Apparently I was wrong."

Wrong? Hellfire, no, she wasn't wrong. She was absolutely right. She was right about him, and she was right *for* him. He was going to pull her up into his arms and tell her so right now.

Unfortunately, someone plowed into him from behind and he went sprawling onto the floor, flailing inelegantly in monumental effort not to land on Miss Langley or any of the puppies. He succeed, but only barely. When he could catch his bearings he realized he was now sitting roughly beside Miss Langley, gazing up at Mr. Skrewd.

"Er... sorry," the curate said awkwardly. "I saw the door open and I thought the puppies might have escaped so I came running. Forgive me, sir, but I didn't see you there."

"So you were planning to meet Miss Langley here," Dovington said.

He was ready for a fight, but the obvious confusion on the curate's face told him there might not be need for that, after all.

"No, I came for... er, is everything quite well, Miss Langley?"

Mr. Skrewd seemed concerned for her, but his eyes were on everything in the hut *but* her. He seemed to be searching for something. Dovington glanced around but couldn't see anything out of the ordinary, other than two grown people and a threesome of extremely happy puppies scattered about the floor.

Pushing past the open door came the mother of the pups. Dovington recognized Bess and she apparently recognized him. She sniffed first the puppies to assure herself of their well-being, then she went to licking the earl straight on his face.

"Were you looking for your dog, perhaps, Skrewd?" he asked.

Miss Langley giggled, and helped pull the shaggy beast off of him.

"No, I... er..."

"He was looking for me."

Dovington could hardly believe his eyes. From behind a

curtain that apparently covered the doorway into what was, most likely, a tiny bedroom, Miss Vandenhoff appeared. She smiled sheepishly and blinked huge, frightened eyes.

"But please don't be angry with him, sir!" she insisted. "It was my idea for us to meet here, not his."

"To *meet* here?" Dovington asked because, for the life of him, he just couldn't make sense of any of this.

Miss Langley appeared just as confused, her face screwed into a puzzled frown as she tried to put her hair and her clothing to rights.

"Why should you be meeting Mr. Skrewd?" she asked. "I thought you were at the ball?"

"I was, but..."

Miss Vandenhoff didn't continue. Her eyes filled up with tears and Dovington knew he'd lost any hope of ever figuring this out. Clearly he'd left rational thought behind when he'd decided to come storming after Miss Langley, so it only stood to reason that he was completely at a loss now. On the floor. In a hut. Covered in puppies.

"Please don't cry, Mable," Mr. Skrewd said to her. "This isn't your fault."

He trod on both of Dovington's legs as he scrambled over them in an effort to get to Miss. Vandenhoff. Miss Langley's skirts may have suffered some treading, too. Eventually, though the curate reached the weeping heiress and things became only slightly more bizarre as she threw herself into his arms. The curate pressed her against his chest and kissed the top of her head.

"Papa wants me to marry the earl," she cried into Mr. Skrewd's shoulder. "But I just can't do it! I don't love him. I love you!"

Dovington glanced at Miss Langley and asked quietly, "Did you know about this?"

"Absolutely not," she assured him in a whisper as the lovers hugged and cooed and reassured each other nearby. "Did you know she thought she was supposed to marry *you*?"

"Er, perhaps I never actually mentioned to her father that Ned would be my stand-in."

She narrowed her eyes at him. "I see. So all this time you've had me trying to manage things for you but nothing was even close to settled already."

"And a fine job of it you've done," he replied, not very much appreciating the tone of accusation in her voice. "Just think how downcast Ned will be when I tell him that—"

But it appeared as if he wouldn't have to tell him anything. Ned was going to see for himself. The young man burst through the door, his boots stamping on the rough floor and his voice booming.

"Skrewd! Where are you? You've got to help me out! I'm desperate, man. My cousin wants—"

He stopped short when his eyes focused in the dim light and his mouth hung open as she took in the scene. He gaped first at the couple in the doorway, then at Miss Langley sitting on the floor in a stunning silk ball gown, then finally at Dovington. It seemed prudent to allow the lad as much time as he needed to contemplate things, so the earl simply stared at him and waited.

"There's a puppy gnawing on your boot," Ned finally stated.

Dovington glanced at his foot. "Yes. So there is."

"Er, why?"

"Because that's what puppies do, man," Dovington replied. "Now why the devil are you here and not at the ball?"

"I needed to see the curate."

"So I gathered. Why?"

"Because... I'm having a crisis of faith."

The curate didn't exactly let go of Miss Vandenhoff, but clearly Ned's statement intrigued him.

"Come in, Mr. Chadburne. I'll help you in any way that I can," Mr. Skrewd said, though Dovington had no idea how there could be any help for any of this.

"It's just that I—" Ned began, then stopped when his eyes went back to the woman wrapped in the curate's arms. "Oh, hello, Miss Vandenhoff."

"Hello, Mr. Chadburne."

The room fell into silence again, so Dovington figured he'd better help the lad out.

"It appears Miss Vandenhoff has professed deep, abiding

love for the curate here, Ned. From the looks of things, he appears in no hurry to rebuff her."

"I'll not rebuff her! I love her," Mr. Skrewd proclaimed.

Now Miss Vandenhoff turned her dewy eyes on Dovington and clenched even more tightly to the curate's narrow shoulders.

"I'm sorry, Lord Dovington," she sniffled. "I tried and tried to be so horrible that you wouldn't want me, but everyone was so nice to me no matter how awful I was. But then I met Ben and I... well, I won't marry anyone but him, no matter what my father says. We'll run away if we have to. That's why I asked him to meet me here now, so we could make plans in case..."

"In case your father made some kind of announcement tonight," Dovington finished for her and rolled his eyes.

It was almost as if he should have expected this. Things seemed to have been going far too easily. He should have known the damn curate would muck this up by...

Wait a moment. If Ben Skrewd was stupidly in love with Miss Vandenhoff, then that meant that he and Miss Langley hadn't been... had they? Was she reeling with heartbreak right now? She didn't appear so. Mostly she was reeling with puppies.

He tried to study her face, to read her expression for any sign that she couldn't care less who Mr. Skrewd might end up married to, but Ned persisted with his interruptions.

"That's exactly why I came here!" he said, almost sounding ready to burst. "I thought I was doing the right thing, Dovey, and I had every intention of doing as you asked, but then you went away and Miss Langley insisted that we all enjoy ourselves and take so many outings and... well..."

"Don't tell me," Dovington stated. "You fell in love."

Ned seemed surprised that he should guess. He nodded. Dovington only hoped that his doleful expression as he gawked down at them did not have anything to do with Miss Langley. When it came to this particular lady, no stand-in was needed.

Or welcome.

"With whom, Ned?" he asked, steeling himself. "Am I going to approve of the match or should I advise you to turn tail and run?"

Ned put his shoulders back and stood very tall. "I'm in love with Miss Renford. And I'd very much like your blessing, Dovey."

Miss Renford. Thank God. Dovington could scarcely recall who that was just now, but it wasn't Miss Langley and that was all that truly mattered. Ned could have any other female on the planet as far as he was concerned. Clearly his plans to save his estate by attaching an heiress were never going to work out, so why not wish the boy happy?

Miss Langley, however, voiced her concern.

"Ella?" she fairly cried. "You wish to marry Ella? But she's too young! And she's not... and you're... surely his lordship is against it."

"No, Miss Renford is a fine young lady and I've nothing against her at all," Dovington said. "But this is hardly the place to discuss such things and my boots are being positively ruined. Why don't we all compose ourselves, then go back into the ball. Surely our absences have been noticed. I'm sure Miss Vandenhoff's father will be much more inclined to favor Mr. Skrewd if he has not been thought to have absconded with her. And Ned... you might want to wipe your feet before going back inside."

Ned glanced at his boots and swore under his breath. Ah, puppies. Dovington asked himself just why he hadn't filled the halls with them at his estate. Were they truly so costly? Too much of a bother? Hell, they were adorable. And the carpets at the Downs were threadbare and motheaten, anyway. By God, his first task when he returned to Surrey would be to find himself a puppy. One just about like these little charmers ought to do.

Susan Gee Heino

Chapter 18

Their guests were abuzz and Mariah did her very best to smile for everyone and pretend to be happy. She stood off to the side and sipped her lemonade, trying to seem very much pleased with the events of the night. The earl had helped smooth things for Mr. Skrewd so he'd gotten the nerve to approach Mr. Vandenhoff and been accepted. He and the heiress were going to be wed.

Ella was dancing with Mr. Chadburne and Mamma had agreed that Mr. Chadburne might officially court her, with the stipulation that there would be no talk of engagement until after Ella's official come-out next year. That seemed to suit everyone, especially the earl.

Mariah tried not to let her skeptical nature fret over the man's intentions at this point. Had he truly given his blessing to his cousin and Ella? It seemed unlikely, considering the previous goal. Was he simply biding his time, hoping that over the course of the coming months the young, starry-eyed Ella would grow weary of Mr. Chadburne and that another eligible heiress might come along for him? Possibly.

What was Mariah to think of it all? With Miss Vandenhoff engaged to be married to their local curate, surely the Vandenhoff family was intending to stay here in this house. The rest of them surely could not stay. But where would they go?

It was hard to enjoy the entertainments of the evening while her mind was swirling with such thoughts.

"Dance with me, Miss Langley," the earl said, causing her to jump as he appeared at her side and whispered in her ear.

"No... I think not sir."

"And why is that? You've gone to so much trouble to make

this event one your neighbors will speak of for months yet to come. You should enjoy yourself."

"Yes, and that's why I would prefer not to dance, thank you."

"Oh. I see. It's like that."

"Like what?"

"You might prefer to dance, but not with me, is that correct?"

"I didn't say that."

"You didn't need to. You've been exhausting yourself trying to appear happy ever since we returned from the hut. Clearly my presence is troublesome for you."

She was not about to let him know just how troublesome it was. She had to keep her composure, find some way to appear unaffected by him.

"I'm simply preoccupied, sir. It is a very big task to oversee a ball, even a small one such as this."

"I wouldn't know, but you seem to have everything well in hand. I daresay your sister has never been happier. Come, dance with me now."

"No!"

Perhaps her refusal had been a bit more forceful than intended. The Bensons were standing nearby and turned to watch them. She wasn't able to produce an actual honest smile, but she did give her best artificial one. The earl was clearly not deceived.

"If you won't dance, then we're going for a walk," he said. "Come."

As usual, he was ordering her around, commanding as if she should simply do as he said and take the arm that he offered. She couldn't, though. Heavens no! She knew only too well how little she could trust her own common sense when in close contact with the man. She didn't dare take his arm or let him lead her anywhere.

"I should stay here," she said quickly. "My mother may have need of me."

"Your mother is find. Ned is busy doting on her and your sister, so I think it's fair to say they will not miss you for a short while."

"But I need to... that is, we shouldn't go—"

142

He interrupted her by apparently going into a spasm and pouring the contents of her lemonade glass all over her gown. She gasped in surprise.

"Goodness, what have you done?"

"Oh, so sorry, Miss Langley," he said loudly, taking her now-empty glass and putting it on the nearest table. "What a looby I am. Here, let me help you."

He took out his handkerchief and would have gone to dabbing at her front if she had not slapped his hand away. She could not have this man pawing at her here, in front of everyone! What was he thinking?

"Come, I'll help you find someone to attend this," he said, taking her by the elbow and ushering her toward the doorway.

She was too shocked by his actions to take note of their direction at first, but when at last she came to her senses she realized he was leading her out of the ball room and into the corridor, not toward the front part of the house that was all lit up to entertain guests, but toward the rear. Where it was dark. Where he had kissed her just a couple hours earlier.

And she realized she was allowing it. She was walking beside him, pretending to worry over the damage to her gown that had already seen the floor of a hut, the antics of puppies, and the bottoms of Mr. Skrewd's boots. This recent splash of lemonade could hardly be cause for concern.

Lord Dovington's actions, however, certainly were. As soon as he got her away from the noise of the dance and any prying eyes that might be around, he stopped. She whirled round to face him, but he had her in his arms long before she had any chance to scold him.

If indeed that's what she'd been prepared to do. At the moment, it was hard to think of anything but letting him hold her and search for her lips with his own. The dim light was no hindrance there. He kissed her long and hard.

Finally he gave her a moment to catch her breath.

"You let me do that, Miss Langley," he said quietly. "Yet you refuse to dance?"

"I... I didn't want people to look at me and to think that... well, they might think I was trying to attach myself to you."

"And that would be so very horrible because...?"

"Because I would never do that, sir."

She hoped he would ignore the fact that she was clinging to him now with such force that a charging buffalo could likely not unattach her. It was too dark for her to clearly read any nuances of emotion in his shadowed expression, but the feel of his arms still tight around her seemed to be a good sign. All she could do was stare up into those midnight eyes and pray she could answer the questions they were asking.

"Is that why you're upset? The thought of attachment, of a connection to me is so very unpleasant for you? My cousin wishes to wed your sister and you can't bear the fact that we share the same bloodline?"

Indeed, she'd not been thinking of his cousin at all, to be very honest. The mention of him in this moment confused her.

"What?"

He put her away from him, holding her at arm's length and studying her carefully.

"I promise you, Miss Langley, he is a good man. He's much better than I have ever been, or likely ever will be. If he loves your sister, and I believe he's convinced that he does, he'll never betray her or give her reason for pain. He will have a slight fortune that will come to him upon his marriage, but I assure you he is not given to excess or waste. If she still wishes to marry him when she comes of age, I pray you don't let his connection to me turn you against him."

"Turn me against him? Of course I would not. How could I? Mr. Chadburne is a good man, just as you say. He's been honest and kind, and he's shown far more intelligence than you have in all of this."

"I'm glad that you... wait, more intelligence?"

"Well, he certainly hasn't been moping around, believing some ridiculous rubbish about what a terrible person he is just because his father was a ne'er-do-well, has he?"

"But his father *was* a ne'er-do-well. He died of drink in the bed of his mistress when Ned was still in leading strings."

"And you'd have him marry *my* precious sister?"

"But he isn't like that! I tell you, he never took after his father, or mine. He's more like his mother's family, and they are excellent people."

"I see. So I take it your mother's people are not."

Now she could see anger in his eyes. He dropped his arms and stepped back from her, ending up in front of a window with moonlight spilling over him.

"My mother was an angel, and her family above reproach. Her father welcomed us when life with my father got to be too difficult for her. Until he died when I was at my first year of school, my grandfather was more parent to me than my father was in all of his life."

"And you repay that by pushing off your responsibility onto your cousin and expecting him to carry the title for you after you're gone?"

"I had my reasons for making that choice, but—"

"They are not very good reasons, whatever they are," she insisted. "Other than this troubling proclivity you show to keep putting your hands all over me, I've found no evidence at all that you are half as awful as you claim."

"Perhaps you don't know me very well."

"I know that you dumped all of my step-father's best spirits out the window rather than drink them."

"That was a colossal error on my part."

"And you didn't raise a finger to prevent your cousin or Miss Vandenhoff from avoiding a match neither of them were, apparently, pleased with."

"Which will no doubt haunt my finances for the rest of my life."

"And you were very gentle with those puppies even though they did dreadful things to your boots."

"You cannot use puppies to argue against me, Miss Langley. I've more than enough shortcomings to make up for a few gentle words here and there. I assure you, there have been more times than I care to recall when I did not dump the spirits out the window but made short work of them, just the same. And if you recall, I was the one who set up the arrangement between Ned and Miss Vandenhoff in the first place, whether they liked it or not."

"Clearly they did not."

"I've been hard-nosed and unpleasant to nearly everyone I know. I've made choices so idiotic they'd make your head swim. Indeed, Miss Langley, it's true. I am my father's son; don't tell me my estimation of myself is inaccurate."

"But it is, and if you had half a brain you could see that," she announced.

"Is that so?" he said. "Well, even without half a brain I've been intelligent enough not to doom myself to spinsterhood simply due to some foolish notion that anyone still cares about the long-ago details of my origins."

"Are you insulting me, sir?"

"No, you do so yourself with mind-numbing regularity, my dear. You carry your bastard status as some sort of badge pinned on your chest, waving it for all the world to see and to condemn. As if there is anything about you that does not scream quality and breeding."

"I have neither quality nor breeding, thank you very much. My mother and I lived in shame and rejection the first years of my life and I can still remember the other children whispering that I had no father. Whispers don't go away, you know. They will follow me forever."

"And you will deny yourself a future, a home, simply because of those whispers?"

"Whose home would have me, sir? No decent person should have to live with that. I should think you would applaud me for not putting my burden on anyone else, for sparing others the shame of my illegitimacy."

He opened his mouth to dispute her, then apparently thought better of it. She had little time to be smug, though. Before she knew it, he'd pulled her into the glow of the moonlight with him and he was wrapping himself tightly around her. Again.

And she loved it.

"The only thing shameful about you, Miss Langley, is the way you feel in my arms," he said. "And I am scoundrel and blackguard enough to keep you here just as long as you're willing."

"If you really were a scoundrel you wouldn't care that I was willing."

But she was. As much as she wanted to deny it, she was hopelessly willing. She hoped he wouldn't notice, but it was likely that he did. The way she pressed herself against him and gazed up into his wonderful eyes, waiting for his kiss, was probably difficult for him to misinterpret.

"So you persist in your claims that I am a decent human being and not well on the road to adding further ruin and disgrace to my family name?"

"I do. You cannot convince me otherwise."

"I say you are wrong. I'm a dreadful person and there is no way I should even contemplate making a life for myself with a wife and a family."

"You could make an excellent life for yourself, if you'd only put your mind to it."

"Is that so? Well, if you are so very certain, Miss Langley, you ought to just marry me to spite me. That would certainly teach me a lesson. You could show me I'm everything you say that I am and then laugh in my face."

"I most certainly ought to, and then... wait, what was that?"

He laughed, cupping her face in his hands and watching her closely.

"Marry me, Mariah. No, don't stare at me like that and try to shake your head. Maybe I am a little bit of an ogre, because I'm not going to take No for an answer."

"But you can't marry me! You know that I'm—"

"Oh, yes, I know that you're stubborn, interfering, and a bit too independent, but I think we can make a go of it anyway."

"No, I was going to say that I'm—"

"I know what you were going to say, and I won't hear it. If you believe I can be redeemed from the disadvantage of my parentage, then certainly you can, too, my dear."

"But..."

"Yes?"

"I'm afraid I can't think of any other reason to refuse you, my lord. I suppose if you don't mind not knowing who my father was, then I certainly don't mind knowing about yours."

"There you see? We sound like a match made in heaven."

147

"Except that I'm not a wealthy heiress."

He shrugged, apparently unmoved by the reminder of their sad financial situation. "You don't need to be. You're already worth a fortune to me."

And that was the sweetest thing he could have said, so she gave up on pretending to be reasonable and pulled his face down toward hers. If he wasn't going to stop talking and kiss her, she was simply going to take matters into her own hands. After all, she really was no lady.

Epilogue

The wedding had been a simple affair, presided over by both the elderly vicar and the newly married Mr. Skrewd. May had bloomed warm and beautiful and everyone in Hinders Sundry said they had never seen a more beautiful bride than Miss Mariah Langley. It did, of course, help that there were not many brides in such a small village and this one was the first to have married an earl.

After the wedding it had been arranged that Ned should escort Mamma and Ella into London to meet his mother and sisters. The Season was still in, so Mamma agreed to stay as guests of Mrs. Chadburne and let Ella come out early if she promised not to complain that her Season was shorter than most. Of course she did not.

The Vandenhoffs had surprised them all. Instead of being disappointed to lose a title for their daughter, Mr. Vandenhoff claimed he'd done better. He'd found the perfect legacy—Mable and her dear curate did not wish to stay in the village, or in England at all. The Vandenhoffs and the Skrewds were going back to New York to use Vandenhoff money to start a foundation for orphans. It would, of course, be named after her father and would be full of good deeds and other important things she approved of.

In appreciation for all of the earl's help in bringing such happiness to Mable and a newfound inspiration for them all, Mr. Vandenhoff paid not only the money he had agreed to for the lease he did not end up taking, but he gifted the lord and his new lady handsomely in honor of their wedding. He also promised to buy his wife a pug.

The money Dovington and Mariah received would be more

than enough to carry them through until the expected income at harvest, and to cover Ella's first Season. It was a welcome surprise and Mable made them promise to visit if ever they happened to turn up in New York. Mariah couldn't imagine what might cause them to simply turn up in New York, but it was nice to know they had friends there if needed.

Everyone had been so eager to get on with their new lives that by the afternoon of their wedding day, Mariah had been left all alone at Renford Hall with her new groom. For approximately five minutes she worried she might be lonely for her mother and sister, but the earl had quickly seen to that.

For the next week they had very much enjoyed not sharing the house with anyone and, in fact, gave the servants quite a bit of free time. By the end of that week, though, it was time to get busy. With practical things. They'd discussed arrangements and things had been settled to everyone's satisfaction.

Ned would take Renford Hall as his home. It was obvious that he and Ella were destined for each other, and Mariah was fairly certain that by the end of this Season, there would be an announcement. Mamma would relent and let them marry early. That would be all nice and tidy and Mamma and Ella would never have to leave Renford Hall. The earl insisted they begin calling it The Grove, but of course no one paid any attention to him on that.

Mariah would be moving to Dovington Downs to take her proper place as Lady Dovington. More good news had come as they'd learned the earl's careful investments had done very well, and coupled with all the other improvements he'd made, they were confident that things were looking up for the Dovington estate. He assured his new wife that with her help and shrewd management abilities, they would likely not starve. She assured him they would do a fine sight better than that and that he'd just best stay out of her way.

On their final day at Renford Hall, a light rain spattered the grounds. The carriages were packed in haste and Dovington urged his bride to hurry along. She did as she pleased but eventually had herself ready and trotted down to the yard to meet him.

"We want to get there while it's still daylight," he said.

"Exactly, so you don't want to have to turn around and come back if I've forgotten anything, do you?"

"Have you forgotten anything?"

"Probably, but I can't think of it now."

She sighed. It was hardly possible to imagine leaving Renford Hall, to never call it her home again. Of course she'd be back to visit, very often, most likely. And Ned promised to consult her if he had any questions regarding the management, but she doubted he'd need her.

Not that she wouldn't have plenty to keep her busy where she was going. Her heart pounded at the thrill of seeing Dovington Downs for the first time. Just think what she could do with a proper estate to look over! Not that the earl didn't already have a very capable steward, and clearly he was more than competent himself to handle his business, but he'd promise to let her be involved in the management of things with him. It was a challenge she could hardly wait to throw herself into.

And the fact that she'd not be alone, that she'd have him right there at her side... it was a dream beyond comprehension. First, though, they had a long ride ahead of them.

"I'm sure I've forgotten something, but I can have the housekeeper send it on, or Mamma when she and Ella return."

"You know, of course, your sister will be married by then. Ned will find some way to convince your mother to let them marry this year."

"If he doesn't, Ella will. But I'm not worried. I've no doubt they will be happy."

"How could they not, if she is anything like her sister?"

She kissed him on the cheek for that and the sly quirk at the corners of his lips told her he thought he deserved much more. He always thought that way, and drat it all, but she usually agreed. Now, however, was not the time.

He pulled the carriage door open for her and ushered her in. She was about to step up, but a call from the yard stopped her. The young boy from the stable was coming round the house and he waved. Mariah waved back and called to him.

"Here, bring them here."

Her husband grumbled, brushing droplets of rain off his coat but waiting patiently. Behind the young man Bess promptly appeared, her black and white coat shaggy with the wet and her three puppies—getting larger every day—came rolling and tumbling along behind her. They were aiming directly for the open carriage door.

"Whoa, wait a moment," Dovington said, a moment too late as all four dogs—and all their mud—leapt up inside.

"We have to take them," Mariah pleaded. "I know only little Bruno was supposed to be yours, but Ella is gone off to London, and Mr. Skrewd couldn't very well take Bess and the puppy he'd selected on that long ocean voyage, could he? I said we'd look after them all."

"There are four wet dogs in my carriage, Mariah."

"I know, my dearest, but you're so gentle with them."

"Four *wet* dogs, Mariah."

"We've blankets. They'll dry."

"It's quite a long drive up to Surrey, you know."

"And you want to be leaving so we get there before dark."

He peered in at the dogs then glanced back at her. She smiled her sweetest for him and knew she had won. He shook his head and held the door open for her again.

"Very well. They may ride in here with us. But," he paused, then leaned in so the boy from the stable couldn't make out his words. "They'd best stay on their own bench. This bench is ours."

And she knew it was going to be an interesting drive, which of course was the perfect way to begin her new life.

Keep reading for a preview of the next
Regency Romance from
Susan Gee Heino...

The Earl's Secret Arrangement
Available 2015

Susan Gee Heino

Chapter 1

Lord Huntley tried to rub the ache out of his throbbing head, but to no avail. The pounding refused to lessen. Likewise, the droning rattle that filled the air around him continued without abate. It was his friend Twillings, nearly shouting at him with incessant ranting. Huntley was still trying to make heads or tails of it.

"And I say you're the most damnable scapegrace, that's what I say," Twillings declared, tapping his walking stick against the hard floor of Huntley's morning chamber as he enunciated each word. "You're the worst sort of sharper, taking what you want when my back was turned and thinking your such a jolly dog for it."

Huntley winced. "By God, Twills, I daresay I'll admit to any crime you wish if it will but shut you up. What the devil time is it, anyway?"

"It is half past ten and time for you to answer for yourself, Huntley."

"I've not yet answered to the ruddy chamber pot," Huntley grumbled. "And where the devil is my valet? He brings me the most miraculous concoction on mornings like this when the gaming went on a bit too deep and the whiskey flowed a bit too easily."

"Celebrating your conquest, were you? Bah! And to think I called you my friend."

"By Hades fire, call me whatever you wish but do it in a whisper. What on God's earth has you in such a lather today?"

"Don't play as if you've no idea of it. You know very well what you did."

"Apparently I do not. At this point, I'm not very well certain what day it is."

"Friday, of course. The morning after you danced two dances with my dearest intended!"

"*Dancing*? Good grief. Is *that* what this is about?"

"It's about a good deal more than dancing, sir."

"Well, if my valet doesn't dance his way into this room with my morning restorative fairly soon, it's going to be about a visit from whatever substance I've got left in my gut."

"I'll not be fobbed off, Huntley! This is a matter of honor. You knew how I felt about Miss Walters, yet you went behind my back."

"And now we are talking of *feelings*? I swear, Twillings, when I find who let you in here at this ungodly hour, I'll--"

"Don't think I'm just some chub, Huntley. I know what you're up to. Admit it: you stole her from me."

"*Stole her?* Wait, you are saying I stole Miss Walters from you?"

"Ah, you remember it now, don't you?"

"I remember going to that dismal ball last night because you begged me to attend with you to meet this goddess of ethereal beauty and endless virtues you claimed to have fallen in love with."

"Miss Walters--she is all those things and more. You met her and saw for yourself what a paragon she is, so you stole her away from me!"

"Well, if I stole her, I can't for the life of me recall where I put her. But see for yourself, I am alone this morning, Twills. Your Miss Walters is not here."

"Good God, I did not say she had run off with you!"

"But if I stole her..."

"You stole her heart, you unscrupulous satyr! I went to her father this morning to declare myself and to ask for her hand."

"Then I wish you happy."

"Don't bother! Her father informed me that she wasn't interested. The magnificent Earl of Huntley had swooped over her like some ravenous bird of prey last night, parading her onto the dance floor and whisking her heart away. It seems she will entertain no suit but yours, you villainous devil, and I was summarily shown to the door."

"What's this? The girl's father thinks I might be turning up to sniff after her?"

"Are you saying your intentions are not honorable? I ought to call you out now, then!"

"Don't get horn mad at me, Twillings. I've no idea where Walters could get this ridiculous misperception. I have no intentions at all for the girl, other than I hope to avoid her like the plague after all this."

"But you danced with her!"

"As did you and half the other men in the room. It was a ball, after all. I was merely being polite toward her, for your sake, damn it."

"Polite, you call it. Predatory, I say."

"*Polite*. And damn it, I should have known better. Just look where all that politeness has gotten me: her father awaiting a proposal and you planning my murder before I've even so much as had a morning coffee. Where is the politeness in that? And, by St. Peter's tunic, where is my blasted valet?"

'I sent him to the devil for you. I'm not leaving here, Huntley, until you have satisfied me that you'll make this right."

"I can't make anything right without my valet and his morning restorative. What the devil has come over you, Twills?"

"I've fallen in love, I tell you. A man in love does remarkable things."

'Ruddy annoying things, you mean."

"I mean to win back my beloved, that's what I mean! You're not worthy of her, Huntley, and I intend to get her back."

"Godspeed in your quest then, lad. Now I wish to win back my valet. Send him in on your way out."

"I tell you, I'm not leaving until you explain how you will relinquish Miss Walters."

"Relinquish the chit? We already established that I haven't got her."

"You've got her heart. Since you clearly have no use for it, then you must devise a plan to release it so that a more deserving man--*me*--can take it up for her."

Huntley rubbed his eyes, wishing he could wake up from this nightmare but finding Twillings still glaring at him once he could focus again. Dash it all, but it was far too early in the day to discuss such things as vital bodily organs.

"I don't care whether you take up her heart or her kidney," Huntley grumbled. "I've no use for either of them and haven't any bloody idea what you expect me to do about this."

"Make her fall out of love with you!" Twillings declared, as if it were the most logical thing imaginable.

"I didn't make her fall *in* love with me! How am I supposed to undo what I didn't do in the first place?"

At this point the chamber door squeaked open and Huntley was overjoyed to see his valet's round face peering in.

"Ah, Mabrey. What a sight for sore eyes. And sore head, and sore shoulders, and sore eardrums. Have you come to rescue me?"

"Of course, sir," Mabrey said, entering the room with a tray and the familiar cup of whatever blessed thing it was he usually gave Huntley after a night too full of pleasure to make for a pleasurable morning.

"And if you don't mind, sir," the valet continued. "I couldn't help but overhear a bit of your dilemma."

"That my head is as large as a walrus and feels just as sluggish?"

"No, not that bit, sir. The part about Miss Walters falling in love with you."

"Ah. That. Well, have you some magical potion in a cup you can offer me for that?"

"I'm sorry, sir, but I'm afraid my solution for that trouble might require more of a hands on approach."

Twillings took definite umbrage at that statement. "His lordship will in no way be putting his hands on Miss Walters!"

This outburst did nothing for the walrus inside Huntley's head. By God, if Twillings did not stop thumping that infernal stick against the floor, Huntley was going to thump it against his ruddy cockloft. Until both items broke.

"I'll be happy if I never set eyes on Miss Walters again," Huntley assured them. "Are you certain she thinks I am interested in her? All I recall is a bit of polite dancing, then I left that deadly dull ball for some cards at my club. Apparently there was a bit of drinking involved after that."

"Likely to soothe your guilty conscience, blackguard," Twillings muttered.

Huntley ignored his friend and turned back to his only source of hope. "Come, Mabrey, out with it. As you can see, I'm in desperate straits. What is your solution?"

"It is just as you said, sir," the valet said, dutifully handing over the cup of blessed restorative. "You have somehow made Miss Walters fall in love with you, so all you need do now is make her fall out of love."

'We've been over this! I can't agree more, but how do I do it, man?"

"It is simple, sir. Why, even a man who intends to maintain a young lady's heart can lose it in one simple step."

Twillings snorted. "Yes, he can allow her to dance with his best friend at a ball."

'Perhaps," Mabrey said with a noncommittal nod. "Or perhaps the lady's heart was not fully engaged to begin with. Are you quite certain you made your feelings known to her, Mr. Twillings?"

"I thought I did, yes. It seemed she felt likewise about me, but—"

"We're not discussing how she felt about *you*, Twillings," Huntley reminded. "It's how she feels about *me* that matters right now and I swear, Mabrey, I'd very much like to hear your thoughts on getting the woman to stop feeling whatever it is that she does feel!"

"It would appear she feels in love with you, sir."

"Then tell me how to make her stop, for God's sake."

"It's quite obvious, sir," the butler explained. "She fell in love with you because she thought you showed devotion to her."

"I was *polite*!"

"Well, then you need to be *more* polite toward someone else. Nothing cools a woman's affection like blatant unfaithfulness, sir."

"Unfaithfulness? What the deuce does that mean?"

"It is a strange, alien notion women have, sir," Mabrey graciously replied. "It goes along with a frightening invention they often call *commitment*."

"I know what it means, man, I simply don't know what you mean by mentioning it at this time."

"I mention it because it is the way you can ensure Miss Walters will stop being in love with you. If she sees you have fallen in love with another, she will no doubt be quite through with you."

"You'd have me break her heart?"

"A hasty knot holds little together, sir. I daresay the damage will be slight when it is undone."

It sounded like a pile of rubbish to Huntley, but Twillings seemed to be taking it all in with approval. He wrinkled his brow, raked a hand through his mussed, sandy hair, and contemplated the valet's words.

"So, you're saying that if Miss Walters thinks Huntley has abandoned her for another, she will give up her affection for him?"

"It is feminine nature, sir, that the young lady will be eager to reattach herself to someone else almost immediately after suffering such a set-back."

But Huntley wasn't convinced. "I thought that when ladies are superseded in a gentleman's attentions they throw themselves onto their couches and languish away from sorrow and loneliness. There is nothing left for them but to wither into haggard, bitter old maids, is there?"

"Oh no, I've heard of that, too!" Twillings exclaimed. "Dash it all, I don't want Miss Walters to languish herself into a haggard, aging wither!"

"No fear," Mabrey assured them. "That sort of thing only happens in ghastly old novels. Miss Walters, I believe, will be far more likely to wish Lord Huntley to the devil, buy herself a new bonnet, and go out to find a fresh beau who will adore her properly."

"And that would be me!" Twillings fairly bounced with gleeful anticipation. "I will be waiting right there to rescue the wounded dove and give safe harbor to her suffering, abandoned soul."

"So you see? The perfect solution."

The valet seemed entirely too smug. The way Twillings beamed and Mabrey preened himself, one might almost think the two of them had come up with a perfect solution, indeed. Huntley, however, would beg to differ.

"Excuse me, but I feel compelled to point out the one obvious flaw in this scheme you're both so very taken with."

"Flaw?" Twillings asked, wrinkling his nose as if the very idea offended him. "There's no flaw in the plan. It's remarkable."

"Yes, remarkable in the fact that neither of you have taken into consideration one very important thing."

Twillings blinked at him in mute confusion, while Mabrey went about preparing his master's clothing for the day, ignoring the mere possibility that he might have overlooked something in his brilliant design. Huntley would take great pleasure in enlightening the haughty creature.

"It might seem worthwhile to point out to the two of you one pertinent detail," he informed them grandly. "I am not, nor do I have any intention of ever being, in love."

Twillings blinked at him. Mabrey paused in his tedious brushing of the already immaculate coat it seemed he had decided his master would be wearing today. Huntley adjusted his dressing gown and smiled at them. Now he was the one feeling smug.

"It is my conviction that being love is a ridiculous state and does nothing but turn an otherwise sensible man into a quivering, useless jelly. No offense, Twillings."

"Taken, sir! How dare you imply that--"

But Huntley was far from dissuaded from his conviction.

"Just look at yourself, man. What of anything you've done or said here today could possibly be construed as not being ridiculous? That's right, you can't think of anything, can you? Indeed. Being in love has made you a sap and I have very little inclination to be a sap. So, I'm sorry to say, I will *not* fall in love with some fortunate female simply to be rid of the one you happen to want for yourself."

Twillings flapped his lips in animated silence, proving

Huntley's point exactly. "But... then I won't... but then we can't... and if you just..."

"If I just what, Twillings? Truly, even if there were some irresistible female I might possibly be inclined to consider falling in love with--and there is *not*--I doubt I could accomplish such a feat in any sort of time frame that might suit your purpose. No, I'm sorry, Twils. I'm afraid Mabrey's plan holds no water."

Twillings raked his sand-colored hair again, looking crestfallen. Mabrey, however, went back to brushing and merely shrugged.

"I don't recall insisting that you do fall in love, sir," he said. "I merely suggested Miss Walters should believe that you are."

"By Jove, that's quite true!" Twillings chirped. "You don't need an actual paramour, just someone that Miss Walters can think you are enamored with... someone she can see you fawning over and courting in public."

"So you would have me play fast with some unsuspecting young lady? No, that is too low even for me. I swear, Twils, this love business has rotted your brain."

"Of course, if the young lady wasn't entirely *un*suspecting..." Mabrey said, carefully laying out a pristine neck cloth and picking at imaginary imperfections in it.

His tone, of course, was casual but Huntley knew he was not to take that for granted. The man's words meant something. His lordship had learned long ago it was in his best interest to pay close attention when Mabrey meant something.

"What is that, Mabrey? You would suggest I court a *suspecting* female?"

"You would hardly be doing a disservice to the young lady if, for instance, she understood your dilemma and had agreed to help out."

"And where, precisely, do you suggest I find such an altruistic young lady?"

He knew, of course, the valet would have a ready answer. He did.

"I have a cousin, sir..."

"You would have me dally with your cousin?"

"Oh, good heavens, no, sir! My female cousins would be far,

far above that."

Huntley chose to ignore that insult and allowed the man to continue.

"I have another cousin--a male cousin, sir--who runs a theatre. I was thinking perhaps he might be able to provide you an actress."

"An actress! Dear Lord, you'd have me parade an actress around town, waving her in the face of respectable women? I think not, Mabrey. Actresses and opera dancers have their place, of course, but a gentleman knows to keep that sort of thing... er, discreet."

"But if no one knew she was an actress, sir--she could play the role of poor relation, or whatnot--people would think it perfectly natural for you to fall in love."

"Pass her off as respectable? Oh, I cannot see how that would go well."

But Twillings was quite taken with the notion. He brightened significantly and began his infernal stick-thumping again.

'It's brilliant, Mabrey! Indeed, if your cousin the theatre man could procure an unknown actress, and if Huntley could manage to pretend to be in love with her, then the scheme just might work! Miss Walters would be off of him, no hearts would be broken, and everything would be put back the way that it should be!"

"Except that you're likely to wind up married at the end of it all," Huntley noted. "Are you certain you're prepared for that?"

Twillings didn't even bat an eye. "Indeed I am. I love Miss Walters and am more than prepared to shackle myself to her for life!"

Huntley shuddered. "As long as the parson doesn't come after me, I suppose I'll agree to your plan. Very well, Mabrey, you may contact your cousin and explain the situation. If he can supply a suitable actress, we will see if this works. Oh, and Mabrey... please specify that the actress understands one thing. I have no intention of actually carrying on with her. Other than the obligatory show for Miss Walters's benefit, I doubt I'll say so much as two words to her."

"Of course, sir."

"And she should have no intention of interacting with society. She must look the part, but we won't want to risk her speaking and ruining the illusion of good breeding."

"Oh, that's wise thinking," Twillings said, rubbing his hands together and nodding as the plan progressed. "Miss Walters must truly believe this is someone worthy of being her rival... someone who could capture an earl."

Huntley agreed.

"Yes, Mabrey, so this actress can be no one the public is too familiar with--or someone who has been too familiar with the public, if you know what I mean."

"I do sir."

"She should be pretty, of course, and tall. Yes, tall would be very nice."

"Blonde, sir?"

"Yes. Blonde would suit well. Insist she is elegant and sedate, too. She should be cool, but not cold."

"The classical Greek-goddess," Mabrey suggested.

"Exactly. People would expect to see me with someone like that, don't you think?"

"And would you have her carved out of marble, sir?"

"Don't be cheeky. It is not every day that a man gets to order up a woman to pretend love with. Besides, people would know right off if I was dallying with a ruddy statue. I'm afraid flesh and blood will have to do in this case."

"Pity for you, sir."

"Yes. A sculpture would be far less likely to rattle my ear off. Make sure she understands, Mabrey, that conversation will not be required. In fact, I would prefer that your cousin selects his most silent actress for our purposes. Can you inform him of that, Mabrey?"

Did the valet just roll his eyes?

"Of course, sir. I'll give all your specifications to my cousin."

"Thank you, Mabrey. I have every faith in you."

"No worry, sir. She'll be just as you like."

"Then perhaps this scheme will not be such a disaster, after all."

Chapter 2

' But this is a disaster!" Hannah Milford declared.

And indeed it was. She'd left tiny Perceval-on-Avon and come all the way to London specifically in hopes of getting help from her cousin as she pursued a career on the stage. What she'd found here instead was a nightmare. Far from being of assistance to her, dear cousin Trudy was in desperate need of assistance herself.

"You can't possibly be pregnant!"

But it was glaringly obvious that cousin Trudy *was* pregnant. Very much so. And worse, she was about to be evicted from her home--Hannah's home now, too. Disaster was too mild a word for their current predicament.

"You should be happy for me, cousin," Trudy said, beaming and glowing and laying her graceful ivory hand over her expanded belly. "By this time next month, I shall be holding my babe in my arms."

"As you sit in the gutter," Hannah muttered. "Good heavens, Trudy, you ought to have mentioned this to me! Did you not tell me it was an excellent time for me to come visit you?"

"Visit me, yes! But gracious, Hannah, I had no idea you meant to run away from your step-father and show up homeless on my doorstep."

"I would have certainly not run away if I'd known there was no place for me to run to! Heavens, Trudy, what are we to do?"

"The landlord can't really be about to put me out of this house," Trudy said, smiling as she sorted a pile of soft linens and tiny buntings. "I've explained to him that Mr. Smith will be returning from his voyage any day now and he will pay all the back rent. Then we'll be married!"

"Trudy... I'm sure you believe your Mr. Smith is a fine enough fellow... but don't you think perhaps it's a bit unrealistic for you to expect him to return after all this time? When did you say he left you, six months ago?"

"Yes, very nearly exactly that."

"And wasn't that just about the time you informed him of your condition?"

"It was."

"Don't you think that perhaps... I'm sorry, but... well, surely you can see how the landlord might just possibly think that you've been... er, abandoned?"

"*Abandoned*? Heavens no. Mr. Smith would never do such a thing. He loves me. The only reason he didn't marry me right away is the fact that he has no money. That's why he left. He went off to make his fortune."

Hannah tried not to let the doubt--no, the *conviction*--show on her face. Even with her own very limited experience in the world she had to admit Trudy's claims seemed remarkably optimistic and naive, to say the least. *Delusional* was actually the more accurate word.

Poor Trudy! Hannah prayed she would not let her cousin see her despair. What was to become of them? And with a tiny new babe... how would they live? Hannah had certainly never been gainfully employed. What could she do?

Cousin Trudy had made her wages on the stage, something she'd not been able to do for months now, not since her condition had developed to the point of being evident and no directors had been inclined to cast her. Bills needed to be paid, though. Trudy may very well have blind faith in her absent Mr. Smith, but Hannah could only be a bit more realistic. They were quite in a pickle.

Hannah had been in such a hurry to leave home when she'd found out what her horrible step-father had planned for her that she'd left all her belongings behind. She'd spent what few funds she'd had on passage to get here and now she had nothing useful to add to their situation. She had nothing to sell and no skills to recommend her. Any girlish hope she'd had of joining her cousin on stage had faded the moment she'd lain eyes on the poor woman's person. Apparently all those warnings she'd heard about girls who ran away for the stage should have been heeded!

"Hannah, please make yourself comfortable," Trudy offered, putting the kettle on to boil as if she had not a care in the world. "I'll make you some tea. Surely you must be exhausted from your journey and here I've been rattling on about myself. Really, you must tell me all about your life these days."

Hannah slumped into the chair Trudy directed her to. It was good to rest after her long journey, but recalling what brought her here could hardly help her relax. Yet here was Trudy, smiling and kind and making her tea. Trudy always had a way of making people at ease around her, apparently even in the most dismal of circumstance. Hannah settled in and began her story.

"What more is there to tell you?" she asked with a weary sigh. "After Mamma died my step-father was eager to be rid of me so he arranged to have me married off to a horrible old man with some land that he wanted."

"How old is he?"

"A hundred, at least."

"And as horrible as that old man who used to chase us from his orchard when we were children and you lived in that little cottage beside Papa's house?"

"Oh, twice as horrible as that."

"Gracious!"

"Indeed. As you can guess, I did not like that arrangement. This is why I invited myself to come visit you. If I'd had any idea how things stood here, however, I'd..."

"You'd what?" Trudy asked. "You'd have stayed in Perceval-on-Avon and married that ogre? No, you did the right thing. We'll take care of you, Hannah. Mr. Smith and I will. You'll be part of our little family."

"Oh, Trudy, I'd love to believe that, but--"

The knock at the door to Trudy's apartments made her jolt in her seat. Her first instinct was to hide. Her step-father had come! He must have figured out where she had gone and he'd come after her! Panic set in and she instinctively leapt to her feet and grabbed up her bag.

But Trudy stayed calm. "Now, now, there's no need to

worry. I told you the landlord was coming by today."

Yes, Trudy had mentioned that, but it did little to lessen Hannah's panic. Perhaps this wasn't her step-father after all, but she saw no reason to let her guard down. A landlord ready to evict them was only slightly less terrifying than a step-father dragging her off to marry an ogre.

Trudy went to the door and opened it wide. Two men stood there. Neither were Hannah's step father and since Trudy smiled and invited them inside, it seemed perhaps this was not a meeting to be feared. Hannah tried to calm her beating heart.

"Good morning to ye, Miss Milford," one of the gentlemen said. "I am glad to see yer looking well."

"Thank you, sir. How nice of you to come by. It is good to see you both."

The men smiled at her, their eyes trained on her as she ushered them into the room. It seemed they had not even noticed Hannah yet. But of course, how could they? Trudy--with her tall, stately form, golden hair, enchanting smile and classical features--outshone everyone.

Not that Hannah minded. Heavens, no. One thing she had always loved about being with Trudy was that people scarcely noticed her diminutive, freckled form above Trudy's brilliance. Hannah had been free to do as she pleased while attention was always on Trudy. It had been quite a satisfying arrangement for them during their younger years, until Hannah's mother had remarried and moved them from their peaceful cottage to her step-father's cavernous home in Perceval-on-Avon. Sadly, all attention had then been on Hannah and she'd not wanted any of it.

But now all those old days returned and Hannah basked in remembrance. Trudy's voice was light and trilled in the air like soft birdsong. Her eyes sparkled for her guests and she swept about her small apartment as if it were a grand palace. Even in her current state Trudy's loveliness drew people to her and the smile that she gave them was infectious. Whoever these men were, Trudy could handle them. They were at her mercy already.

"Gentlemen," Trudy began. "You must meet my cousin, just arrived in Town. Miss Hannah Milford, these are dear friends of mine. This is Mr. Skrewd and his cousin, Mr. Mabrey."

Finally the men noticed Hannah. She smiled, though of course it was nothing like a smile from Trudy. The men were polite and both bowed for her. Clearly their attention was all on Trudy, however. The one man--the one Trudy called Mabrey--seemed overly prim and proper in appearance yet he could barely keep from staring at her.

"Mr. Skrewd is the owner of the Babylon Gate Theatre," Trudy explained, indicating the other man, far more rumpled and less prim than his cousin. "Where I have been working these recent years. He is also the very generous owner of these apartments here. Doesn't he keep a lovely building?"

"He's your landlord?"

"The sweetest, dearest one in all of London," Trudy said.

Poor Mr. Skrewd was clearly flustered by all the smiling and sugary words. Trudy was very good at that, as Hannah well knew. If the man had come here to evict them, Trudy was not making it easy for him.

"But have you come on business, Mr. Skrewd?" Trudy asked, her huge eyes suddenly welling up and blinking rapidly at the gentleman. "I'm afraid Mr. Smith has not yet returned with the rent for you, and I know that I did promise to pay you right away, but as I've not been able to be on the stage due to my delicate condition..."

"Er, well yes... that is why we're here," the man began, clearing his throat multiple times and glancing nervously at his companion. "Mr. Smith has certainly been absent a while now and you must know there are expenses for keeping a building such as this one..."

"Oh, but you keep it so very well!" Trudy gushed. "And you ve been so very patient with me. I can't thank you enough, Mr. Skrewd. I was just telling Miss Milford what a dear, dear soul you are. I know if there was any way you could help me in my hour of need, you certainly would."

Hannah was beginning to worry that Trudy might be troweling the flattery just a bit thick at this point, but Mr. Skrewd's words proved that even in her *delicate condition*, the actress had not lost her touch.

"And that's why I've brought Mr. Mabrey," the landlord said quickly. "I mentioned to him your, er, situation and he has an offer that might help you out."

Hannah didn't much like the sound of that. She knew enough to know that the offers of men were not always as helpful as they sometimes purported. Trudy, more than anyone, should know that by now. Still, here were two men with some sort of offer and here was Trudy smiling sweetly and gullibly at them.

Mr. Mabrey, however, seemed suddenly hesitant to continue.

"I'm not sure, cousin, that this will work, now that I see... now that I give further thought to the situation."

"Oh, please, Mr. Mabrey," Trudy prodded. "You must tell me what Mr. Skrewd is talking about. Why have you come here today?"

Mr. Mabrey cleared his throat and held himself very upright, as if he were addressing the queen herself.

"I have come here today in search of an actress to play a specific role for a short time."

Trudy fairly glowed with excitement. "Ah! Well, that is exactly what I am, sir; an actress. And as I have only a short time before I must confine myself, it appears I am perfect for your role."

Mr. Mabrey, however, did not appear to share her enthusiasm. Hannah could well understand why. It was easy enough to see from the man's pained expression when he looked at her that Mr. Skrewd had failed to inform his cousin just how far advanced dear Trudy's condition was.

"I'm afraid, Miss Milford," Mr. Mabrey began. "That you are not as perfect for the role as I had hoped. To be blunt, I was hoping for someone a bit less, er, expectant."

Trudy waved her hand and dismissed his silly concern. "The child will not fall out unceremoniously, sir. I have weeks yet to go. And I assure you, I'm a master at costumes and concealment. Once I'm on the stage, from a distance no one will suspect at all."

"But that's the trouble," Mr. Mabrey went on. "This role will not be played from a distance. It will require, er, close personal contact."

Just as Hannah suspected. Oh, the nerve of these men!

Assuming that just because a woman was not the most respectable sort--and clearly Trudy was not--she would be willing to do all manner of even worse things just to pay her rent. Well, it was a good thing for Trudy that Hannah was here. She would defend her poor cousin, most certainly.

"I am quite sure that my cousin has no wish to play *that* sort of a role, sir," Hannah interjected. "I don't know what you think of her, but truly you have misjudged. She may be an actress, and she may have been abandoned in a sorry state by her Mr. Smith, but I promise you that she is far above accepting whatever so-called role it is that you offer her now."

Both men seemed surprised to recall that she was even in the room, let alone to hear her speak. They turned their focus on her now, Mr. Mabrey, in particular, sizing her up.

"You are new to London?" he asked.

"I am, sir. I've come from Perceval-on-Avon to visit my cousin and it appears I've come at just the right time."

"You speak your mind, don't you?"

"I see no reason not to, sir, especially when the well-being of someone I care for is at stake."

Mr. Mabrey's eyes narrowed. Apparently he did not approve of ladies who expressed their opinions or stood up for their loved ones. Well, she did not approve of men who would take advantage of desperate women. Or who narrowed their eyes and glared at her as if she were an insect under dissection.

"I note you have red hair, miss," the man commented.

"I prefer the term auburn."

"And you are not tall."

"Nor am I a rhinoceros. Now if you'd please get back to the business at hand, I'm sure you will find my cousin has no intention of involving herself in the sort of role that you offer."

"Oh, don't be too hasty, Hannah," Trudy said quickly, leaping in before Mr. Mabrey had opportunity to scold Hannah for her rudeness. "We should hear Mr. Mabrey out. Surely he is not suggesting what he seemed to suggest. Are you, Mr. Mabrey? You would never come to insult me with anything but a legitimate stage role, of course."

"I am afraid the role is a bit unconventional, Miss Milford..."

Hannah restrained herself from jabbing a finger in the man's chest and yelling "Ah ha!" She couldn't, however, remain silent.

"So you admit it! Well, I'm sure my cousin thanks you for your time, but her answer is No."

"How unconventional, sir?" Trudy asked, ignoring Hannah's outburst.

"Rather, miss," the man replied to her, not quite taking his disapproving gaze off of Hannah, though. "But nothing dishonorable, I assure you."

"No, it's quite a gem of a role, actually," Mr. Skrewd piped up. "You'd get paid a pretty penny, and not have to lift yer skirts or nothing like that."

Hannah gasped at the man's frank language and Mr. Mabrey cringed, but confirmed his cousin's assertion.

"Indeed, there would be nothing at all of that nature involved. Strictly respectable and for a very limited time only."

"Would the role be here in London?" Trudy asked.

"Oh yes, it would be in London."

"And the pay?"

"More than enough for the back rent," Mr. Skrewd announced.

Trudy smiled. "Well, then. What would I be doing?"

Hannah couldn't believe her ears. Was Trudy truly willing to consider whatever it was these gentlemen offered? Good heavens, but things must be even more desperate than she knew. Poor, poor Trudy.

Mr. Skrewd seemed thrilled that his tenant was so willing to cooperate. He replied eagerly to her questions, his smile nearly as bright as Trudy's.

"You'd be taking leisurely drives in the park, wearing elegant clothes, enjoying the opera, that sort of thing. The whole point of this role is to be seen happily about Town with a very fine gentleman of quality. Nothing more."

"Oh, that sounds delightful!"

Hannah shook her head. "No, it sounds even more disreputable than ever. What sort of legitimate role would require a lady to do these things, sir?"

"This one does," Mr. Skrewd said. "What say you, Trudy.

You up for it?"

"Certainly!"

"But she doesn't even really know what *it* is yet!" Hannah protested.

"And there is, of course, the small matter of her, er, condition," Mr. Mabrey added.

Mr. Skrewd grumbled. "It's true. I should have told you Trudy's condition was rather advanced, but surely you can see she'd do a bang-up job of it nonetheless, cousin. Ain't she pretty enough? And tall, like one of them Greek godesses, just like you said your master insisted on. She's even blonde, ain't she? Come now, yer master told you to hire the girl at the earliest moment, so let's make the arrangements."

Trudy smiled and Mr. Mabrey studied her. Finally he seemed to come to his decision and he nodded at his cousin.

"Very well. With one stipulation."

"What is it?" Mr. Skrewd asked.

"I won't hire this Miss Milford," Mr. Mabrey said, indicating Trudy. "But I will hire the other one."

About the Author

Susan Gee Heino thinks the sexiest thing a man can do is engage in witty banter. If he happens to be wearing breeches and a cravat while he does this, all the better. If he comes with a noble title, a tortured past, and perhaps even dimples, then he is just about perfect.

Her lighthearted Regency Romances are full of quirky heroines who tend to feel exactly the same way—at least they do by the end of the book. Usually it takes a little convincing by the cravat-clad hero. But no matter what adventures ensue, the hero always ends up with his lady. And vice versa.

Ms. Heino lives in rural Ohio with her non-cravat-inclined husband, two very remarkable children, and an accidental collection of critters. She loves to hear from readers so please visit her website or connect on social media!

www. SusanGH.com
Love's funny sometimes!

www.ingramcontent.com/pod-product-compliance
Lightning Source LLC
Chambersburg PA
CBHW070548180626
46817CB00005B/1747